THE ASSASSINS OF ROME

Caroline Lawrence

The Roman Mysteries: Book IV

THE ASSASSINS OF ROME

ROARING BROOK PRESS
Brookfield, Connecticut

Published by Roaring Brook Press
A Division of The Millbrook Press,
2 Old New Milford Road, Brookfield, Connecticut 06804
First published in 2002 in the United Kingdom by Orion Children's Books, London

Library of Congress Cataloging-in-Publication Data
Lawrence, Caroline.
The assassins of Rome / [Caroline Lawrence].—1st ed.
p. cm.—(The Roman mysteries ; bk. 4)
Summary: Flavia and Nubia follow Jonathan to Rome and into the Golden House built by the emperor Nero, where a dangerous assassin lurks.
1. Jews—Rome—History—Fiction. [1. Jews—Rome—History—Fiction.
2. Murder—Fiction. 3. Titus, Emperor of Rome, 40-81—Fiction.
4.Rome—History—Empire, 30 B.C.-476 A.D.—Fiction. 5. Mystery anddetective stories.] I. Title. II. Series.
PZ7.L429As 2003
[Fic]--dc22 2003016880

ISBN 0-7613-1940-9 (trade edition)
2 4 6 8 10 9 7 5 3 1
0-7613-2605-7 (library binding)
2 4 6 8 10 9 7 5 3 1

Printed in the United States of America

First American edition 2003

To my son Simon,

the realist

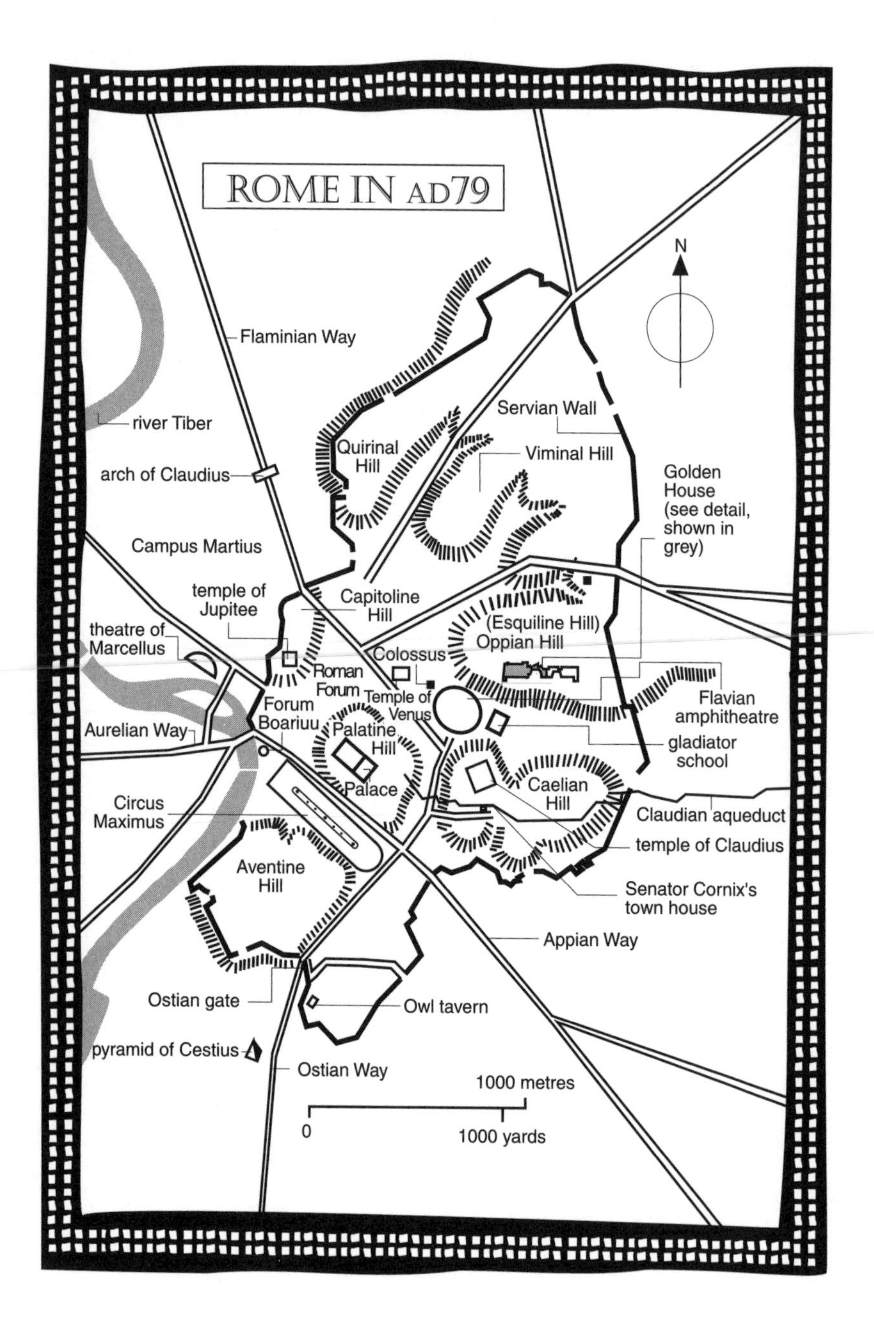

ROME IN AD79
N
Flaminian Way
river Tiber
arch of Claudius
Campus Martius
Servian Wall
Quirinal Hill
Viminal Hill
Golden House (see detail, shown in grey)
temple of Jupitee
Capitoline Hill
theatre of Marcellus
(Esquiline Hill) Oppian Hill
Colossus
Roman Forum
Temple of Venus
Forum Boariuu
Flavian amphitheatre
Aurelian Way
Palatine Hill
gladiator school
Palace
Caelian Hill
Circus Maximus
Claudian aqueduct
temple of Claudius
Aventine Hill
Senator Cornix's town house
Appian Way
Ostian gate
Owl tavern
pyramid of Cestius
Ostian Way
1000 metres
0
1000 yards

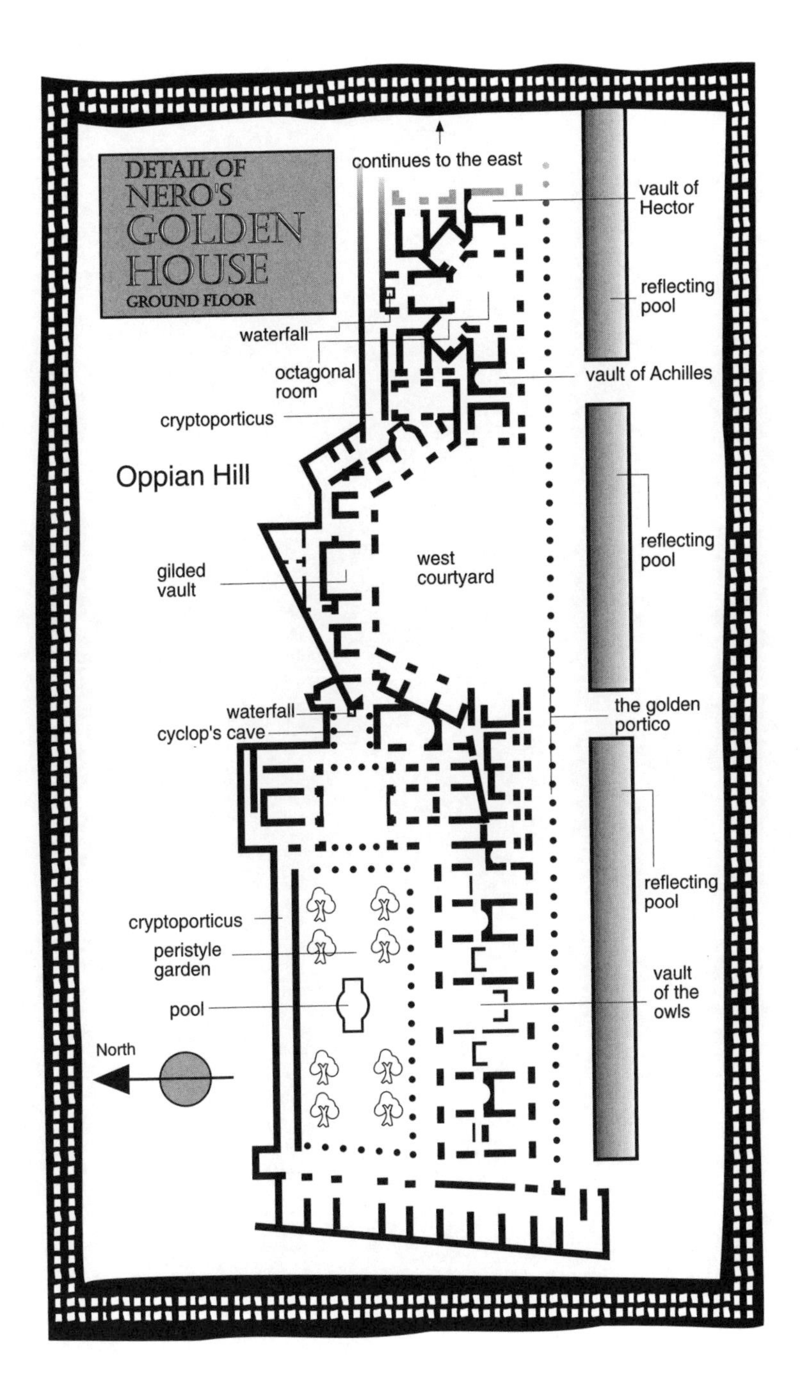

DETAIL OF NERO'S GOLDEN HOUSE
GROUND FLOOR
continues to the east
vault of Hector
reflecting pool
waterfall
octagonal room
vault of Achilles
cryptoporticus
Oppian Hill
reflecting pool
west courtyard
gilded vault
waterfall
the golden portico
cyclop's cave
reflecting pool
cryptoporticus
peristyle garden
vault of the owls
pool
North

THE ASSASSINS OF ROME

SCROLL I

One hot morning in the Roman port of Ostia, two days after the Ides of September, a dark-eyed boy stared gloomily at four presents.

The boy and his three friends sat on cushions around a low octagonal table in a small triclinium. It was a pleasant room, with cinnabar red walls, a black and white mosaic floor, and a view through columns into a green inner garden. A faint sea breeze rustled the leaves of the fig tree and they could hear the fountain splashing.

"I'm telling you," said the boy. "Something bad always happens on my birthday."

"Jonathan," sighed his friend Flavia Gemina. "In the past month you've survived a volcanic eruption, a coma, and capture by pirates. But now you're safe at home and it's a beautiful day. What could possibly happen? Don't be such a pessimist."

"What is sessimisp?" asked a dark-skinned girl in a yellow tunic, taking a sip of pomegranate juice. Nubia was Flavia's former slave girl. She had only been in Italia for a few months. Although Nubia was a quick learner, she was not yet fluent in Latin.

Flavia drank some of her own pomegranate juice. Then she held out the ceramic cup.

"Nubia," she said. "Would you say this cup was half empty or half full?"

Nubia studied the ruby-red liquid and said, "Half full."

"Then you're an optimist. An optimist always looks on the bright side of things. What do you think, Jonathan? Is it half full or half empty?"

Jonathan glanced into Flavia's cup. "Half empty. And it's not even very good pomegranate juice. It's too sour."

Flavia grinned at Nubia. "See? Jonathan's a pessimist. Someone who always expects the worst."

"I'm not a pessimist," said Jonathan. "I'm a realist."

Flavia laughed and handed the cup to the youngest of them, a boy in a sea-green tunic the same color as his eyes.

"How about you, Lupus?" she asked. "Would you say the cup is half full or half empty?"

"He can't say anything," said Jonathan. "He's got no tongue."

"Shhh!" said Flavia. "Well, Lupus? Half full or half empty?"

Lupus tipped the contents of the cup down his throat.

"Hey!" Flavia protested. But they all laughed when Lupus wrote on his wax tablet:

COMPLETELY EMPTY

Lupus grinned but did not look up. He was writing something else on his tablet, using a brass stylus to push back the yellow beeswax and expose the wood beneath. He showed it to Jonathan:

OPEN PRESENTS!

"All right, all right," said Jonathan. "I'll open yours first."

He picked up a grubby linen handkerchief tied with an old piece of twine and weighed it in his hand. "It's heavy. And knobbly. And . . ." Jonathan tipped the contents onto the octagonal table. ". . . it's rocks. You gave me rocks for my birthday."

"They're not just any rocks," said Flavia. "Lupus searched a long time for those."

Lupus nodded vigorously.

"They are smooth and round and perfect for your sling," explained Nubia. She held one up. "See? Now open my present." She placed a twist of papyrus into Jonathan's hands.

Jonathan undid the papyrus and pulled out a leather strap. "A dog collar?" he said with a frown. "So you can take me for a walk without worrying that I might run off?"

"My present is for you and for Tigris," said Nubia. "Maybe more for Tigris."

"Thanks, Nubia." Jonathan gave her a wry smile and showed the collar to his puppy, Tigris, who was gnawing a lamb bone beneath the table. "And thank you, too, Lupus. Rocks and a dog collar. This morning I got an abacus from Miriam and a new cloak from father. Useful presents all around." He sighed.

"Well, I know you'll like my present," said Flavia, handing Jonathan a blue linen bag. "It's not useful at all."

"Hmmn. A present from Flavia. I wonder what it could be? It's the same size and shape as a scroll. And surprise, surprise—it is a scroll. *The Love Poetry of Sextus Propertius*?" Jonathan raised an eyebrow at Flavia. "Isn't that the scroll you told me you wanted?"

"Was it?" Flavia grinned sheepishly. "No, but I think you'll really like it, Jonathan. There's a wonderful poem about a beautiful girl with yellow hair just like you-know-who."

Jonathan made a sour face, put down the scroll, and examined the blue bag it had been wrapped in.

"I do like this bag though," he said, in a more cheerful tone of voice. "I could use it to keep my nice sling stones in."

"Oh, you can't have that," said Flavia, unrolling Jonathan's new scroll. "It's Pater's. I just needed something to wrap it in."

Jonathan sighed again. "Who's this one from?" He reached for the last present, a small pouch of yellow silk.

Flavia looked up. "That's from you-know-who," she said. "From Pulchra. And from Felix. Pulchra asked me when your birthday was, and they gave it to me before we left."

"Now this . . ." said Jonathan. "This is a nice present."

In his hand he held a small jar with black glazed figures on apricot-colored clay.

"Pulchra told me the vase is from Corinth," said Flavia. "It's called an alabastron. It's very old and fabulously expensive."

"Everything in Pulchra's house is fabulously expensive," said Jonathan dryly. But he looked pleased and showed it to the others.

"Look, Nubia," said Flavia. "It's a scene from the poem we were studying in lessons this morning. Odysseus and three of his companions. They're putting out the eye of the Cyclops with a sharpened stick."

"Great Neptune's beard!" exclaimed Nubia. "Why are they doing that?"

"Because he's a huge, ugly old giant who's planning to eat them," said Jonathan as he started to pick the yellow wax away from the cork stopper.

Flavia nodded. "Remember how Aristo told us it took Odysseus ten years to return from Troy? Polyphemus the Cyclops was one of the monsters Odysseus faced on his journey home."

"I remember," said Nubia. "Odysseus is the hero whose wife is always weaving and unweaving."

"That's right," said Flavia. "Everyone thought Odysseus was dead and all the men wanted to marry Queen Penelope so they could become king. But she was a faithful wife and never gave up hope. She said she would marry one of her suitors as soon as she finished weaving a carpet. But every night she lit torches and undid what she had woven by day. She was sure that Odysseus would return."

"Happy birthday, little brother!" Jonathan's beautiful sister, Miriam, came into the dining room and set a platter on the low table. "I've baked your favorite sesame seed and honey cakes. But you can only have a few. Otherwise you'll spoil your appetite for later."

"Thanks," said Jonathan. He popped a cake into his mouth and offered the plate to the others.

"Miriam," said Flavia, taking a bite of her sesame cake, "is it true that something bad always happens on Jonathan's birthday?"

Miriam looked thoughtful. "Now that you mention it . . . See this scar on my arm?" She pushed back the sleeve of her lavender tunic to show them a barely visible mark just above her left elbow. "That's where Jonathan shot me with an arrow on his eighth birthday."

"That was an accident," said Jonathan with his mouth full. "But remember how I fell out of the tree at our old house last year and was knocked unconscious and Father made me stay in bed all afternoon?"

Miriam nodded. "And on your birthday the year before, you ran outside to try out your new sling and stepped right on a bee."

"It wasn't a bee." Jonathan reached for a third honey cake. "It was a wasp."

Miriam gently slapped his hand and picked up the platter. "Jonathan's foot swelled up like a melon and he couldn't walk for three days," she said over her shoulder as she took the cakes out of the room.

"Yes." Jonathan sucked the honey from his fingers and reached for the alabastron again. "Something bad always happens on my birthday. And it's usually my own . . . Oops!"

Suddenly the room was filled with a heady fragrance. The little jar lay in pieces on the black and white mosaic floor. Tigris sniffed at the pool of spreading oil.

"Oh, Jonathan," said Nubia. "You dropped the bottle of Pulchra."

"And it was filled with scented oil," said Flavia. "Wonderful scented oil."

Jonathan was silent. He stared miserably at the broken jar and the golden oil seeping into the spaces between the small black and white chips of marble.

"Quickly!" cried Flavia. "Mop it up. Save it." She pulled Jonathan's linen handkerchief from his belt and pressed it to the glistening oil. Then she used her own. Nubia did likewise. Lupus looked around and grabbed the handkerchief he'd wrapped the stones in. As he got down on his hands and knees to wipe up the last of the oil, Tigris licked his face.

"What is that scent?" Flavia closed her eyes and inhaled deeply. "It's not balsam or myrrh or frankincense."

"I know I've smelled it before," said Jonathan. "It makes me feel so sad."

"How can it make you feel sad?" Flavia said. "It's a wonderful scent. It makes me feel . . . excited."

"It makes me feel freedom," said Nubia solemnly.

Lupus took his wax tablet and wrote:

LEMON BLOSSOM

"Of course," said Jonathan. "It's the perfume they make from their citron tree at the Villa Limona."

For a moment they were silent, as they recalled the beautiful villa on the Cape of Surrentum and the events of the previous month. Despite their encounters with pirates and slave-dealers, each one of them had special memories of the Villa Limona, its owner Pollius Felix, and his beautiful daughter Pulchra.

"Maybe we'll return there one day," said Jonathan, staring out between the red and white columns of the peristyle into the leafy inner garden. The others nodded.

"Felix was so generous," sighed Flavia. "He gave me that Athenian drinking cup, and he gave you the bottle with scented oil and he gave Nubia a new flute." She tipped her head to one side. "Lupus, did Felix ever give you anything? He liked you best."

Lupus patted out a beat in the air with the flattened palms of his hands.

"That's right," said Flavia. "He gave you a drum."

Lupus stopped air-drumming and reached for his wax tablet. He smoothed over his previous words with the flat end of his stylus, then wrote a new message:

HE IS LOOKING FOR SOMETHING ELSE

"For you? He's looking for something else to give you?" asked Flavia.

Lupus nodded.

"What?" asked Jonathan.

Lupus shrugged and looked down.

"Well," said Flavia, pushing a strand of light brown hair behind her ear, "Whatever it is he's looking for, I'm sure he'll find it. Felix is even more powerful than the Emperor."

"I wouldn't repeat that statement," came a voice from outside the dining room. "Emperors have been known to kill people for saying such things!"

SCROLL II

"Doctor Mordecai!" cried Flavia.

Jonathan's father stood in the doorway of the triclinium. Dressed in a loose blue caftan with a black sash and turban, he blocked some of the light from the garden.

"Peace be with you, Flavia and Nubia." Mordecai bowed to the girls and as he stepped into the room it grew brighter again. "It is not wise even to hint that someone might be as powerful as the Emperor," he said gravely. "Less than a year ago Titus killed a man who suggested he should not be Emperor. And I'm sure you would not want any harm to come to Publius Pollius Felix. He proved to be a most valuable friend—dear Lord." Mordecai sat heavily beside the girls. "That smell."

"It's lemon blossom," said Jonathan in a small voice. "I broke a perfume bottle."

"I have not smelled that scent in nearly ten years."

"Where do you know the smell from?" Jonathan looked at his father.

Mordecai was silent for a moment. Flavia could see where his beard had been singed by a hot wind from the eruption of Vesuvius.

"In Jerusalem," said Mordecai at last, "in the courtyard of your grandparents' house. A beautiful lemon tree grew there. Your mother loved that tree. The only scent she ever wore was lemon blossom."

"Oh, Jonathan," said Flavia. "That's why the scent makes you sad. It makes you think of your mother." She tried to swallow the lump in her throat.

"But I was only a baby when we were separated," Jonathan said. "How could I remember her perfume?"

"The sense of smell is the first and most primitive of all our senses," said Mordecai. "I doubt if you remember your mother's face, and yet you remember her scent. As do I," he added quietly.

Flavia's eyes filled with tears. She couldn't remember her mother's face either. She had been three years old when her mother died giving birth to twin baby boys. Thinking about her mother reminded Flavia of her father, the sea captain Marcus Flavius Geminus. He had left on a voyage before the volcano erupted and there had been no news of him since. Flavia told herself he was fine and would soon be home, but a hot tear rolled down her cheek and she had to bite her lower lip to stop it trembling.

There was a sniff to her left and Flavia saw that Nubia's cheeks were also wet. Nubia's father had been killed by slave-traders and the rest of her family led off in chains.

Lupus's eyes were dry, but red-rimmed. He seemed to stare through the garden and into the past.

"I never realized it before," said Flavia. "But we all have something in common: None of us have mothers."

"That's right," murmured Jonathan and glanced up at Mordecai. "Father?"

"Yes, Jonathan?"

"Why did Mother die?"

"I've told you before. She was killed during the siege of Jerusalem nine years ago."

"I know *how* my mother died. But I want to know *why* she died.

Why did she stay behind in Jerusalem when we got away? Why didn't she escape with us?"

Mordecai lowered his eyes. "Your mother's father was a priest. He said it would be unseemly for his daughter to flee the city. She chose to obey her father rather than me."

"But didn't she mind that you took Miriam and me with you? Didn't she love us?"

His father was silent.

"Father?"

Mordecai lifted his head but he did not meet Jonathan's gaze. "Of course she loved you," he said briskly. "She loved you very much. But I insisted on taking you and Miriam with me. At least she obeyed me in that."

Flavia looked sharply at Mordecai. She sensed he wasn't telling them everything. And she could see Jonathan was dissatisfied with his answer, too.

Suddenly Tigris barked and scampered out of the dining room. The next instant Flavia heard pounding at the front door, followed by Miriam's voice, sounding worried. A moment later Miriam appeared in the doorway, her face even paler than usual.

"Soldiers," she whispered, her violet eyes huge with alarm. "Two soldiers and a magistrate are here to see you, Father!"

Three men stood in the atrium of Jonathan's house: two burly soldiers and a short man in a white toga. Tigris had planted himself at their feet and was barking steadily up at them. Next door, in Flavia's house, Ferox, Scuto, and Nipur had begun to bark in sympathy. Soon all the dogs in Ostia would be at it.

"Tigris! Be quiet!" Jonathan picked up his puppy and scratched him behind his ear. "Good dog."

"Peace be with you." Mordecai gave the men a small bow. "Every stranger is an uninvited guest. May I help you?"

"Doctor ben Ezra," said the man in the toga. He was young, with thinning hair and light brown eyes. "We meet again."

"Bato!" cried Flavia. "You're Marcus Artorius Bato, the magistrate. Remember me? You helped us catch a thief a few months ago."

"Of course I remember. You're Flavia Gemina." A half smile passed across his face and then he frowned at their tear-stained cheeks and red eyes. "Has someone died?" he asked.

Jonathan nodded. "Our mothers," he said.

Bato's frown deepened as he studied their four very different faces. Then he gave his head a little shake, as if to clear his mind.

"Doctor," he said, turning his pale eyes back to Mordecai. "We have reason to believe that a dangerous criminal may be on his way here. Do you know a man called Simeon?"

"Simeon?" said Mordecai.

"Simeon ben Jonah." Bato consulted his wax tablet. "A ship from Greece docked this morning and the suspect was seen disembarking. Our informant recognized this man Simeon and followed him long enough to hear him ask where the Jewish doctor lived. As far as I know, you are the only Jewish doctor here in Ostia."

Jonathan glanced at his father as Bato continued, "Apparently this Simeon is extremely dangerous. We believe he's an assassin. Do you have any enemies, Doctor? Anyone who would hire someone to kill you?"

"No. That is, I don't think so. . . ." Mordecai's face was pale.

"Well, I suggest you bolt your door. And don't go out without a bodyguard. We have men out looking for him but if you like, I can assign a pair of soldiers to guard your house."

"Er . . . no. No, thank you. That won't be necessary," said Jonathan's father. "We will be careful."

"Another mystery," exclaimed Flavia. "How exciting!"

"It's not a game." Bato frowned at her. "This assassin is dangerous."

"What is sassassin?" whispered Nubia.

"Someone hired to kill people," replied Flavia under her breath.

"What does he look like?" asked Jonathan.

Bato flipped open his wax tablet again. "Our informant says Simeon is about thirty years old. Tall, slim, and dark. Has a beard and long frizzy hair. Exceptionally long hair, which may be hidden by a turban." He turned back to Mordecai. "I'm sorry. My notes are brief. Obviously, if you see anyone of that description lurking about—"

"We will inform you at once," said Mordecai.

"Has he killed many people?" said Flavia quickly, as the magistrate turned to go.

"Yes, he has. According to my notes." Bato hesitated. "In fact, his name is on a list of known assassins whom we have orders to arrest on sight."

The four friends glanced at each other in alarm.

"We'll be careful," said Mordecai and held the door open for Bato and his soldiers.

As soon as they left, Jonathan turned to his friends. "Wonderful," he said. "A deadly assassin on his way to murder us. No, nothing bad ever happens on my birthday!"

SCROLL III

"Nubia, how many days has Pater been gone?" said Flavia.

The two girls had been to the baths and were resting in their garden until it was time to go next door to Jonathan's birthday dinner party.

Nubia was lying on her stomach underneath a bubbling fountain. "We are sailing in the boat of your father to the farm of your uncle," she said. "Then two days after, we are carting to Pompeii to see your father sail away again. The night before, there is no moon."

"That's right," Flavia murmured. She was sitting on the marble bench in the shade of the fig tree, making marks on a wax tablet. "Pater sailed from the harbor of Pompeii on the day of the new moon. And tonight's the new moon again."

Nubia turned back to look at the dust at the base of the fountain's marble column. She was watching some black ants struggle to push a grain of barley up a small anthill. Nearby, under the jasmine bush, Ferox, Scuto, and Nipur panted like three sphinxes in a row: one big, one medium, and one little.

"That means Pater's been gone exactly a month," sighed Flavia, putting the tablet down on the shade-dappled bench. "It seems like so much longer."

"Many things happen," said Nubia, keeping her eyes on the ants.

"I know," said Flavia. "The volcano, Jonathan almost dying,

Miriam falling in love, the pirates . . . That's why I'm going to keep a journal. I don't want to forget anything that's happened. Maybe I'll ask Lupus to illustrate it."

Nipur gave a gentle whining yawn and thumped his tail; he was getting bored. But Nubia was fascinated by the four ants who were still trying to maneuver the barley grain into their anthill. As the barley rolled away for the third time, Nubia decided to help.

Carefully, with the tip of her forefinger, she nudged the barley up the mound and left it poised at the very opening. Presently the ants found it and waved their feelers with excitement. Then they tipped the grain of barley into the cool depths of their ant home and disappeared after it.

Nubia smiled and rolled over onto her back. Now the ants would have their banquet and sing tiny ant songs, never dreaming that a huge creature loomed above them and took an interest in their fate.

She sighed. The splashing of the fountain and the rhythmic buzz of the cicadas in the umbrella pines was making her drowsy. She closed her eyes.

Abruptly, she opened them again. Next door, Tigris was barking his alarm bark.

Jonathan walked downstairs very slowly, one step at a time. When they had moved to Green Fountain Street a few months earlier, one of the items he remembered unpacking was his mother's yellow jewelry box. His father had forbidden him to look inside.

As Jonathan reached the bottom of the stairs, he caught a whiff of the lemon perfume, which still lingered in the triclinium. He paused for a moment, to make sure he hadn't been noticed. Tigris wasn't barking any more: Lupus was playing with him in their bedroom. His father was in the study with the gauzy curtain drawn, which meant he was studying Torah. Miriam was the one to worry about. He had to pass the kitchen, where she was preparing his birthday dinner.

Jonathan slipped off his sandals and left them at the bottom of the wooden stairs. He wished he could be more like Flavia: She never felt guilty when she disobeyed her father.

Jonathan took a deep breath and walked. Thankfully, Miriam had her back to him; she was kneading dough and singing in Hebrew.

With a sigh of relief, Jonathan slipped into the storeroom, leaving the door open just enough to admit a beam of dusty light.

Cautiously, he picked his way between the half-buried amphoras of wine, dried fruit, and grain. In the dimmest corner of the storeroom were some wooden shelves. His mother's jewelry box was on one of these, up high. But he was tall enough to reach it.

The box was wooden, with a vaulted top and a flat bottom, painted in a glaze of clear yellow resin and decorated with red and blue dots in neat rows. Jonathan examined it for a moment in the bar of light from the doorway. At last he found the catch. What he had taken for the bottom was actually the lid. It slid open smoothly to reveal some jewelry and a small papyrus scroll tied with a yellow cord.

Jonathan's heart was pounding. He shouldn't be doing this, but he had to know why his mother hadn't escaped with them. He had a nagging suspicion that it had been his fault. That was why his father had never told him the real reason she stayed in Jerusalem.

Jonathan examined the jewelry first: a silver necklace with pendants of green jasper, some plain silver thumb bands, and what might have been a nose ring. There was also a signet ring.

The stone was sardonyx, the same color and transparency as a nugget of dried apricot. It had a dove carved into it. Jonathan tried the ring for size and managed to squeeze it on the little finger of his left hand.

Still wearing the ring, he picked up the small scroll. It wasn't a continuous strip, but several sheets of papyrus rolled together. He was able to slip out the innermost sheet without undoing the knot in the cord.

The sheets were yellow with age. They must be at least ten years old. Maybe fifteen.

"How much more pleasing is your love to me than wine," Jonathan read in Hebrew, "and the fragrance of your perfume than any spice. With one glance of your eyes, Susannah, you have stolen my heart."

The scraps weren't signed but Jonathan knew they must be love letters from his father to his mother. The handwriting looked like his father's, but it was stronger, bolder, more vigorous.

Jonathan felt his face grow hot. It was hard to imagine his father as a bold young man in love. Jonathan scanned the other sheets, but they were also love letters. Nothing there. Nothing to indicate why his mother hadn't come with them when they left Jerusalem. What had he expected to find? He tried to swallow, but disappointment filled his throat.

Carefully, he rolled up the sheets of papyrus and slipped them back into the knotted cord. Then he frowned, and sniffed the roll. Lemon. Faint but unmistakable.

"Mother," he whispered. "Why didn't you come with us? What did I do wrong?"

He was about to put the jewelry box back on the shelf when he remembered the ring on his little finger. He tried to pull it off, but in vain. The day was very hot and his hand was sticky. Never mind. He would hold his finger under the fountain for a few moments and put a drop of olive oil on it to help it slide off.

As Jonathan crept out of the storeroom and eased the door shut behind him he frowned. Why were men's voices coming from the study? Surely his father was alone?

He took a step closer. Now he could see his father's turbaned head through a gap in the gauzy curtain. Mordecai was sitting on the striped divan beneath the scroll shelves. His head was in his hands.

"Of course she's dead," Jonathan heard his father say in Hebrew.

"And it's my fault. As her husband, I should have insisted she come with us."

"No, no," came a deep voice, as low as a lion's purr. "She'd made up her mind to stay. Because of Jonathan. It wasn't your fault."

Jonathan's heart pounded. "Because of Jonathan." He'd been right. It was his fault. But who was the man? Jonathan took another cautious step. As he moved forward, the man sitting next to his father came into view. In the garden a bee buzzed among the lavender and he could hear Miriam singing softly in the kitchen.

The man sitting next to his father had a dark beard and frizzy hair so long it fell over his shoulders.

Jonathan's blood went cold.

Simeon.

It could only be Simeon the assassin.

Jonathan opened his mouth and yelled.

SCROLL IV

"Help! Assassin!" Jonathan yanked aside the study curtain. The man leaped to his feet but before he could run away or pull out a weapon Jonathan head-butted him in the stomach.

"Ooof!" The tall man collapsed on the floor.

"Quick, Father!" Jonathan looked around for something heavy. "Hit him while he's confused!"

"It's all right, Jonathan!" Mordecai cried in Hebrew. "He won't hurt us."

The long-haired man lay gasping on the floor.

"Simeon! Are you all right?" Mordecai's prayer shawl slipped to the floor as he bent to help the man to his feet. The man groaned and lifted his big head. Jonathan found himself looking into a pair of amused blue eyes.

At that moment there was the sound of running feet and barking puppy. Lupus and Tigris raced into the study. Lupus was brandishing Mordecai's curved sword.

"Stop!" cried Mordecai in Latin. "It's Jonathan's uncle!"

Lupus skidded to a halt.

Tigris, however, did not understand Latin. All he knew was that his master was in danger and there was only one possible threat. With a fierce growl, Jonathan's puppy leaped forward and sank his sharp teeth into the stranger's ankle.

■■■

"Simeon is your uncle?" Flavia stared at Jonathan as he dried his hands on a linen towel. Jonathan nodded. It was early evening and they had all gathered for his birthday dinner party.

"Why didn't you tell us?" asked Flavia.

"We didn't know ourselves," said Miriam, pouring a stream of water over Nubia's hands. "He arrived this morning while we were having lessons at your house. Apparently Simeon was upstairs asleep in Father's room when the soldiers arrived. I didn't recognize the name Simeon; I always called him Uncle Simi."

"And I was just a toddler, too young to remember him at all," said Jonathan.

"Then your father lied to Bato?"

"He had a good reason. Uncle Simi is on an important mission. No one must know."

Flavia's eyes opened wide. She lowered her voice: "But Bato said Simeon was—"

"—an assassin?" A tall man with long dark hair followed Mordecai into the dining room. He had intense blue eyes above his dark beard.

Flavia swallowed and nodded.

"Flavia," said Jonathan, "this is my Uncle Simeon. Simeon, these are my friends Flavia and Nubia."

Simeon nodded at the girls and sat cross-legged beside Jonathan on an embroidered cushion. Instead of reclining on couches, Jonathan's family preferred to sit on the floor.

"Are you sassassin?" asked Nubia, her amber eyes wide.

"I am . . . a messenger," said Simeon. "With important information for the Emperor Titus." Simeon leaned forward to hold his hands over the copper bowl while Miriam poured water on them.

"But you're Jewish like us," said Jonathan. "Don't you hate Titus for destroying Jerusalem? Because Father said, I mean . . . Is it true you were in Jerusalem when Titus destroyed it?"

"Yes," said Simeon quietly. "I was there."

"Will you tell us what happened?" asked Flavia.

■■■

"I was nineteen years old when Titus sacked Jerusalem," began Simeon. The candles had been lit and Mordecai had pronounced the blessing. Now Miriam was passing round the first course—a tray of hard-boiled eggs—while Lupus filled the cups with well-watered wine.

Nubia frowned. "How did Titus sack Jerusalem?"

"I think you mean 'why,'" said Mordecai. "Jerusalem and Rome have long been enemies, mainly for religious reasons."

"But how?" persisted Nubia. "Titus is not a very big man." Nubia had seen the Emperor a few weeks earlier at the refugee camp south of Stabia.

"He had four legions with him." Simeon dipped his egg in the mixture of salt and chopped coriander, then sniffed it reverently before biting into it. "Legions," he repeated at Nubia's blank look. "Five and a half thousand soldiers per legion plus as many auxiliaries. That makes nearly fifty thousand men."

"Oh," said Nubia, and nodded solemnly. "But what did he do with the sack?"

Simeon almost smiled. "To sack a city means to kill the defenders, carry off valuable objects and enslave the people who live there."

"Oh," said Nubia again. "You must have been afraid."

"It was unspeakably awful. There was a famine. No food," he explained quietly, lowering his eyes. He had thick eyelashes, and despite his long face there was something appealing about him. He reminded Nubia of a sad puppy and she had the sudden urge to pat him on the head.

Simeon continued: "There should have been food enough to feed everyone for ten years, but some of our own people destroyed the grain stores. They thought it would force us to come out of the city and fight the Romans. But it didn't work. Within a few months the food was gone. Soon we began to eat horses, mules, and dogs. Finally we resorted to sandals, belts, even rats."

Nubia shuddered and Flavia put down her half-eaten egg.

"When Titus's legions finally broke through the walls and took the city, it was almost a mercy," said Simeon. "His soldiers killed the weak and the old and they enslaved the rest of us. Some were thrown to animals in the arenas. Others were taken to Rome for Titus's triumphal procession; to be paraded and then executed. I was one of those sent to Corinth to join thousands of other Jewish slaves working on Nero's isthmus."

"What is ithamus?" asked Nubia.

"An isthmus is a deep ditch joining two seas so that ships can sail through. It cuts months off their journey time."

"Pater sails through the Isthmus of Corinth all the time," said Flavia to Nubia, and turned to Simeon: "Our tutor Aristo comes from Corinth. Do you know him?"

"I doubt it," said Simeon. "We Jews have our own camp outside Corinth. Though it's more like a town now. We've been there many years."

Miriam rose to her feet. "I must get the stew before it gets cold," she said. "Lupus, can you bring the bread?"

Lupus nodded. He and Tigris followed Miriam out of the dining room. They were back a moment later: Miriam with a big ceramic bowl, Lupus holding a fat round loaf.

"It's venison, lentil, and apricot stew," said Miriam, setting the bowl on the low octagonal table. "With cumin and honey. It's Jonathan's favorite. Get down, Tigris! Or Jonathan will have to shut you in the storeroom."

They tore pieces of bread from the loaf and used them to scoop up the sweet stew straight from the bowl.

"Wonderful!" Simeon closed his eyes. "Ever since those terrible days of hunger in Jerusalem, I never take even a dry crust of bread for granted. But this! This is sublime."

"It is delicious, Miriam," said Flavia, and everyone else nodded.

Nubia noticed that Jonathan had hardly touched his food. "Uncle

Simeon," he said slowly, with a glance at his father. "Why did you stay in Jerusalem? Why didn't you escape when we did?"

"I was a Zealot, a freedom fighter," said Simeon. "I was young and wanted to fight Romans. We called those who left cowards, but I wish now. . . . You were right, Mordecai. In the terrible days that followed I often cursed myself for not listening to you."

Mordecai nodded sadly.

Jonathan gave Tigris a piece of gravy-soaked bread. "Simeon," he said. "Was my mother with you in Jerusalem?"

"Yes, of course," said Simeon. "Susannah was my younger sister."

"What happened to her? After Titus sacked Jerusalem."

"I don't know. I was telling your father earlier that they separated the men and women. There was terrible confusion. It was the last time I saw her alive."

"Do you know why she stayed? Did she ever tell you why she didn't?"

"Jonathan." Mordecai's expression was grim. "Please don't pursue this subject. I told you already why she didn't come with us."

Nubia saw the injured expression on Jonathan's face. He hung his head and stroked Tigris. Suddenly the puppy stiffened and gave a single bark. A moment later they heard pounding on the front door.

"You must hide at once, Simeon," hissed Mordecai, as Miriam ran to answer the door. "It may be the magistrate again."

SCROLL V

'It's not the magistrate, Father. It's Gaius." Miriam held the hand of a tall, fair-haired man.

Everyone breathed a sigh of relief and Mordecai turned to Lupus. "You can give Simeon the signal to come out now."

"Did you find a house, Uncle Gaius?" asked Flavia.

Her uncle shook his head. Despite his broken nose and a scar across one cheekbone, Flavia still thought him very handsome.

Gaius smiled down at Jonathan.

"I'm sorry I'm late for your dinner party, Jonathan. Happy birthday!" He extended a flat wooden object painted with red and blue stripes. "It's just a wax tablet but I thought you might like the stripes."

"I do," said Jonathan reaching to take it. "Thank you. It's very . . . useful."

"Jonathan!" cried Flavia. "You've hurt your finger!"

A strip of white linen was wrapped round the little finger of his left hand.

"It's nothing," Jonathan flushed and put his hand under the table.

Mordecai gave his son a sharp look, but at that moment Lupus and Simeon came back into the dining room.

"Gaius," said Miriam, "this is my Uncle Simeon."

After the introductions had been made and Miriam had

washed Gaius's hands, they tucked into the venison stew again.

"It looks lovely on you," said Gaius.

"Thank you," Miriam whispered, and blushed as everyone looked at her. "My new tunic," she explained. "It's a present from Gaius." The long tunic was white linen, edged with a narrow gold border.

Simeon looked at Miriam. "It's been nearly ten years since I saw you last," he said slowly. "You have become a great beauty, like your mother." He looked at Gaius. "You are very blessed."

"I know," said Gaius, without taking his eyes from Miriam.

"Have you set a date for the wedding yet?" asked Simeon.

Gaius shook his head and dipped his bread in the stew. "I won't set a date until I've found somewhere for us to live. And that reminds me . . ." He looked up at Flavia. "Tomorrow I must go to Stabia. I have some unfinished business with Felix and I want to see whether it's possible to rebuild the farm."

Flavia and Nubia glanced at each other. Soon after the eruption, they had looked down on the remains of Gaius's farm from a nearby mountain ridge. It had been almost completely buried by ash.

Suddenly Lupus grunted and held up his hand.

"What is it, Lupus?" asked Flavia.

Lupus put his finger to his lips and widened his eyes.

In the silence they all heard the noise: a distant moan coming from the direction of the sea. Then came several short blasts, followed by a long mournful note again.

"It makes the hair on the back of my neck all prickly," said Flavia. "What is it?"

"It is sounding like a horn," said Nubia.

"It's the shofar," said Miriam. "A trumpet made from a ram's horn. And that means it's time for our last course." On her way out of the dining room, Miriam glanced up at the darkening sky. "Yes. I can see three stars. The first day of the new year has begun." Flavia saw her give Gaius a radiant smile before she went out toward the kitchen.

SCROLL VI

Jonathan was coming back up the stairs from the latrine when he noticed a light flickering in the guest bedroom.

"Lupus?" he whispered, looking in.

"No," said his Uncle Simeon. "Just me." He sat on the side of his bed. A flickering oil lamp on the low table made his shadow huge on the wall behind.

"What are you doing?" asked Jonathan, wide-eyed. His uncle held a kitchen knife in one hand and a mass of frizzy hair in the other.

"I'm cutting off my hair," said Simeon in his deep voice.

Jonathan stepped into the room.

"Uncle Simeon," he said. "Please tell me about my mother. I have to know."

The blade gleamed in the dim lamplight as Simeon lifted the knife toward his head. Another long strand of dark hair fell onto the bed. "They say long hair is a disgrace to a man," he said. "But when I was a Zealot, we always considered it a mark of bravery and courage."

"Uncle Simeon. I just dreamed about my mother. I dreamed she was alive."

His uncle's head snapped up.

"You what?" He slowly lowered the knife.

"I dreamed she was weaving in a cave. And in my dream she told me she was still alive."

"Dear God," whispered Simeon, and even in the dim lamplight Jonathan could see him grow pale.

"What? What is it?" asked Jonathan.

Simeon looked up at him. The lamp lit his face from beneath and made it look like a mask. "Jonathan. As you know, I'm on my way to Rome to see the Emperor. Even though my mission is urgent, I came via Ostia specifically to see your father and tell him something of great importance. He is not ready to hear. But perhaps . . ." Simeon laid the knife beside the oil lamp, ". . . perhaps you are the one I was meant to tell. Jonathan. Are you prepared to believe something extraordinary?"

"Yes." Jonathan sat on the bed next to his uncle. "Tell me."

The next day dawned hot and still. Nubia saw that the sky was a curious color, a green so pale it was almost white.

She watched Flavia's Uncle Gaius peer up at it, too, as he slung his travel bag over his shoulder.

"It's going to be very hot today," he observed. "As hot as the days of the Dog Star." He unbolted the front door and stepped out into the early morning street.

"Aren't you going to say good-bye to Miriam?" Flavia stood beside Nubia.

He shook his head and glanced at the house next door. "It's a special day for them today. Miriam and I said our good-byes last night." He turned back, kissed Flavia on the forehead, patted Nubia on the head, and set off toward the harbor with his faithful dog Ferox limping along beside him. Nubia knew he intended to sail to Puteoli and from there to Stabia.

The girls watched him go out of sight, then went back in and carefully bolted the door behind them. Because the first day of the Jewish New Year was a day of rest for Jonathan and his family, there were no lessons that morning. Their tutor, Aristo, had taken the day off to go hunting with a friend.

Nubia spent most of the morning listening to Flavia read the Odyssey in Latin. They sat in the shadiest corner of the garden but even there the heat soon became almost unbearable. They had just reached the part about the return of Odysseus when the door slave Caudex showed Miriam into the garden. Nubia immediately knew something was wrong. Miriam's eyes were red and she was hugging Tigris tightly in her arms.

"Jonathan's disappeared," said Miriam. "Simeon's gone, Lupus hasn't come back yet, and . . . and Father's been arrested."

"Drink this barley water, Miriam," said Flavia in her calmest voice. "And tell us what happened."

Miriam was sitting on the marble bench between Nubia and Flavia. Scuto and the puppies lay panting beneath the jasmine bush.

"Just before dawn," said Miriam, "Father and I were called out to see a patient: a woman near the Laurentum Gate in the final stages of labor. We managed to save her, but the baby died." Miriam took a sip of barley water and looked at Flavia. "That always upsets me."

"I know," said Flavia gently. Nubia patted Miriam's shoulder.

"When we got back a short while ago, the house was empty. Jonathan and Uncle Simi were nowhere to be seen. And we haven't seen Lupus since he ran off last night."

"Maybe Jonathan is seeking Lupus," suggested Nubia.

"I don't think so," said Miriam. "If Jonathan had gone looking for Lupus, he would have taken Tigris."

"Jonathan's been acting strangely." said Flavia. "Last night, he told me your father hates him. He thinks it's his fault your mother died."

Miriam stared at Flavia. "Of course it wasn't his fault. And Father loves Jonathan terribly."

"I know," said Flavia. "But that's not how he feels. Did anything else happen after we left last night? Anything at all?"

"There was something," said Miriam slowly. "Late last night something woke me. I think it was Jonathan crying out in his sleep. Then, just as I was dropping off again, I heard him talking to someone."

"Who?"

"It wasn't Father, so it must have been Uncle Simi."

"Did you hear what they were saying?"

"No. Maybe I only dreamed it."

Flavia fanned herself with her hand. "Even if he is upset, it's not like Jonathan to run off. Lupus, yes; but Jonathan, no. You're sure he didn't leave a message?"

"He might have," said Miriam. "Father and I were just about to look for one when that magistrate Bato and his two big soldiers knocked on the door. This time they looked angry. They searched the house and they found . . ." She began to cry.

"What?" said Flavia, "What did they find?"

"They found some strands of long hair in the kitchen. Uncle Simi must have cut it off and tried to burn it on the hearth. But he didn't burn it all, and Bato said it was evidence. Then he arrested Father."

"Oh Pollux!" muttered Flavia. She stood up and walked to the fountain. "Maybe . . ." she said slowly, "maybe Simeon and Jonathan saw the soldiers coming and went to hide somewhere. We'd better go next door to your house and look for clues."

"We can't just look for clues!" There was a note of hysteria in Miriam's voice. "They may be torturing Father!"

"Don't worry," said Flavia. "I don't think they torture freeborn people, only slaves. There's no point any of us going to the basilica, anyway. They'd never listen to girls. Oh, I wish Uncle Gaius were here. He could talk to the magistrate."

"Gaius won't be back for at least a week," said Miriam.

"I know," said Flavia, and then: "What about Aristo? Miriam, you wait here in case Aristo gets back early from hunting. If he does, tell him what's happened. He can go to the forum and find out about your father. Meanwhile, Nubia and I will see if Jonathan left a message at your house."

"I don't want to be on my own," said Miriam in a small voice.

"Alma and Caudex are here. And the dogs," said Flavia. "Look! Here comes Alma now with more barley water. Alma, will you look after Miriam?"

"Of course," said Flavia's former nursemaid, a cheerful, well-padded woman. "Would you like to help me shell peas, Miriam?"

Miriam gave a small nod.

"Thanks, Alma," said Flavia. "Come on, Nubia. Let's look for clues."

Flavia found Jonathan's wax tablet lying open on Mordecai's table in the study. She recognized the red and blue stripes on the edge. She lifted it carefully because the late morning sun pouring on to the desk had melted the soft beeswax. Only the top part of the message, still in the shade, was legible.

And that was in Hebrew.

"Yes, I can read it," said Miriam a few minutes later. They had brought the tablet carefully back to Flavia's house. Miriam was sitting in the shady part of the peristyle shelling peas with Alma. Flavia slid the wax tablet onto the table.

"No! Don't touch it!" cried Flavia, as Miriam reached for the tablet. "Jonathan left it open so your father would see it, but the sun melted the wax. If you tip it, the liquid wax will cover up the letters."

"All right," said Miriam. She leaned forward. "The message says: 'Gone to Rome. Please . . .'" Miriam looked up at them, her violet eyes wide. "That's all there is," she said.

"Can't you make out anything else?" said Flavia. "Is that a word there?"

Miriam bent her curly head over the tablet. "It might be

'Simeon,'" she said after a moment. "But I'm not positive."

"That's strange," said Flavia, pacing back and forth in the shade of the peristyle. "Why would Jonathan suddenly go to Rome? And what does it have to do with Simeon?"

Then she stood as still as a statue. "Maybe," she said slowly, "maybe Simeon really is an assassin and an enemy of your father's! What if he kidnapped Jonathan as revenge and forced him to write this message? Or somehow tricked him into going away with him?" Despite the intense heat, Flavia shivered. "If Simeon is just a messenger as he told us, why does he need Jonathan? Oh Pollux! This really is a mystery." She left the shade of the columned peristyle and walked to the fountain.

"Too hot to think," she muttered, and took a long drink from the cool jet of water. "Plan, plan, need a plan . . ." She wiped her wet mouth with her hand, then splashed some water on her face and the back of her neck. "We have to find Jonathan and help him."

Abruptly she stopped, then slowly turned. "Nubia," she said, with a gleam in her eye, "how would you like to visit the Eternal City?"

SCROLL VII

Just inside the arch of Ostia's Roman Gate was a long stone trough where the cart drivers watered their mules. Several tall umbrella pines cast their cool shadows over the trough and the area around it. In this shady patch stood a small altar to Mercury, a folding table, and several benches.

The cart drivers had their own tavern and stables just behind the trough, and their own baths complex across the road, but after they had bathed and filled their stomachs, this was where they waited for their next fare to Rome.

It was almost noon, and only two drivers still sat at the table, playing knucklebones and watching the world pass by. Above them—in the high branches of the umbrella pines—the cicadas buzzed slowly. The heat was ferocious. Even in the shade, the men were sweating.

"I've never known it so hot after the Ides of September," Flavia heard the bald man say to his friend.

"Blame the mountain," said the other man, whose short tunic revealed the hairiest legs Flavia had ever seen. "Ever since it erupted the weather's changed. Seen the sunsets?"

"Who hasn't?" Baldy reached for his wine cup. "And this morning the sky was green. They say it's going to be a bad year for crops. There's talk of drought."

"There's already a blight on the vines." Hairy Legs tossed his knucklebones on the table and winced.

Baldy made a sour face, too, as he tasted his wine. "The vintage can't be any worse than what we're drinking now," he said, putting down his cup. "This stuff tastes like donkey's—"

"Ahem!" Hairy Legs cleared his throat loudly and indicated the girls with his chin.

"Can I help you girls?" said Baldy.

"Yes, please," said Flavia politely. She was wearing her coolest blue tunic and a wide-brimmed straw traveling hat, but already rivulets of sweat were tickling her spine. "We'd like a lift to Rome."

The two men glanced at each other with amusement.

"I have the fare," said Flavia, standing a little taller. "I believe the standard rate is twenty sestercii."

"That's right." Hairy Legs picked up his knucklebones and tossed them again. "Venus or nothing," he muttered to Baldy, and to the girls: "I suggest you come back tomorrow morning, girls. Best time is just after dawn."

"But we have to go today." Flavia tried to keep her voice low and confident.

Hairy-legs glanced up at her. "You sometimes find drivers leaving a couple of hours before dusk," he said. "But those are mostly delivery carts."

Flavia knew that if they waited till dusk she'd have to ask Aristo's permission. And he might not give it.

"We have to go as soon as possible," she said, but her resolve was already beginning to falter. Maybe they shouldn't rush off to Rome, a tiny voice seemed to be saying. Lupus still wasn't back. Miriam was on her own. It was an extremely rash thing to do.

Baldy tutted. "It's noon," he said. "The hottest time of the day on the hottest day of the year. Only a madman would set off for Rome in this heat."

"Or someone with an urgent delivery for the Emperor," said a voice behind them.

Flavia and Nubia both turned to see a young man in a brown cart driver's tunic. He had round green eyes, a snub nose, and short, spiky brown hair. He reminded Flavia of a cat.

"What are you talking about, Feles?" said Baldy, with a laugh. "Since when are you delivering to the Palatine Hill?"

Feles ignored Baldy. "I can see you're a girl of good birth," he said to Flavia with a polite smile. "I'm just off to Rome. Taking a load of exotic fruit that can't wait. It's not a big load and I've got some extra space. If you don't mind a rather cramped journey I'll take you for only ten sestercii."

"Um . . . well . . ." began Flavia.

"Now she's changed her mind." Baldy laughed and shook his head. "Just like a female."

Flavia glared at him and turned to Feles. "Of course we'll accept your kind offer."

"Good," said Feles. "It'll be nice to have some company. My cart's just there by the trough. If we—who's this?" he said, as Caudex lumbered up to them gripping a satchel in each hand.

"It's our bodyguard, of course," said Flavia. "You don't think we'd be foolish enough to go up to Rome on our own?"

"Been to Rome before?"

Flavia shook her head. She sat beside Feles at the front. Nubia and Caudex rode in the back of the cart, shaded by a canvas tarpaulin.

The carriage had rolled slowly out of Ostia down an oven-hot deserted road. First they had passed between the tombs of the rich and then, as these thinned out, the salt flats on either side, thickly bordered with reeds and papyrus. Presently the road rose up on a sort of causeway. Beside it towered the red-brick aqueduct that brought water from the hills to Ostia. The road ran steadily alongside it and presently both road and aqueduct left the marshes behind and began to pass scattered farmsteads surrounded by melon and cabbage patches. Beneath the arches of the aqueduct were small vegetable gardens, as colorful as patchwork blankets.

Flavia glanced back at Nubia and Caudex. They were leaning against wooden crates and facing the open back of the cart. Flavia could just see Nubia's shoulder and arm. In the crates was a fruit Flavia had heard of but never seen. Oranges. Their color was beautiful and their scent divine. Flavia had asked to try one, but Feles said they were worth their weight in gold.

"Twelve crates, each with forty oranges, that's 480 pieces of fruit. If even one's missing, I could feel the sting of the lash."

Now Feles was asking her about Rome.

"Going for the Ludi Romani? Plan to watch a few chariot races? See a few plays?"

Flavia shook her head, and gripped the side of the cart as they rocked over a bump. "No, we're visiting relatives."

"Well, make sure you see a race, as it's your first time in Rome. And don't miss the new amphitheater. Titus is trying to finish it in time for the Saturnalia, but I don't think he'll do it. Even with two thousand slaves working dawn till dusk."

Feles uncorked a water gourd with his teeth and had a long drink. Then he offered it to Flavia. She took a drink of water from the gourd and handed it back. Feles shook his head. "Let Nubia and the big guy finish it. There's a tavern and a fountain by that row of cypress trees up ahead. I can refill it there and we'll have a little rest."

Flavia passed the gourd back to Nubia and squinted against the sunlight. She could just make out dark, flame-shaped smudges floating above the shimmering waves of heat that rose up from the road.

"The trees look like they're up in the air," she said.

"Trick of the heat. Like what you get in the desert. Right, Nubia?"

"Yes. Like desert." A voice from the back of the cart, barely audible above the clipping of sixteen hooves on the stone-paved road.

"How did you know Nubia comes from the desert?" asked Flavia.

"It's obvious, isn't it?" Feles grinned. "But I am a bit of a detective. I could tell you were high-born the moment I saw you. And I know the big guy used to be a gladiator by the way he stands."

"That's right!" said Flavia. "Feles, have you heard of a man called Simeon? Simeon ben Jonah?"

"Name sounds Jewish," said Feles.

"It is."

Feles laughed. "Well," he said, "you'll have your work cut out for you if you're looking for a Jew in Rome. You know those two thousand slaves I mentioned?"

"Yes . . ."

"They're all Jewish. Titus captured them when he took Jerusalem a few years ago. No, wait. More like ten years now. Doesn't time fly?"

Flavia frowned. "I thought Titus sent the Jewish slaves to Corinth."

"Yes, some went to Corinth. But there were plenty to go around. Titus brought the strongest and handsomest back here to Rome," Feles chuckled to himself. "And the prettiest . . ." he added.

"What do you mean?"

"Those Jewish women," said Feles, shaking his head in admiration, "are the most beautiful in the world." He gave Flavia a sideways glance and added proudly. "My girlfriend's one. She's lovely. Huldah's her name. She's a slave girl in the Imperial Palace on the Palatine Hill."

Flavia twisted her whole torso to face him. "Then some of the women from Jerusalem are in the Imperial Palace?"

"About two hundred," said Feles, "all of them high-born." He mopped his brow. "This heat. Never known it so hot. How're you doing back there?" he called.

Caudex grunted and Nubia said, "We are doing fine."

"We'll stop for a break soon," said Feles. "Then you can change places."

The cart rolled on and presently tall cypress trees on the left threw bands of delicious shadows across the white road. The mules quickened their pace. They smelled water and green shade up ahead.

"This tavern's roughly the halfway point to Rome," said Feles. "See the milestone? Seven miles. It'll take us about two more hours."

Later, standing in the shade of cypress and pines, drinking cool water from the fountain, Flavia took Nubia aside.

"Nubia," she whispered. "Did you hear what Feles told me? There are lots of female slaves from Jerusalem in Titus's palace. One of them might know how Jonathan's mother died. And if I figured that out, so could Jonathan."

SCROLL VIII

After their short stop at the tavern, Nubia took her turn beside Feles at the front, and Flavia joined Caudex in the back. The road was climbing more steeply now, and the line of the aqueduct guided Flavia's eye back down to Ostia and the red brick lighthouse—minuscule at this distance—with its dark plume of smoke rising straight into the dirty blue sky.

They passed through woods of poplar, ash, and alder. Presently Ostia was hidden from view. On any other day the tree-shaded road would have been deliciously cool. But today Flavia's blue tunic was soaked with perspiration and clinging to her back.

"Caudex?" Flavia whispered because the big slave's eyes were closed.

He didn't reply and presently she too dozed fitfully, occasionally jolted out of sleep when the cart left the deep ruts in the stone road and rocked from side to side. The rumble of the cart was louder back here and she was glad the wheels weren't rimmed with iron, like some.

She dreamed briefly at one point. She was hunting with Jonathan and Nubia among the tombs outside Ostia. In her dream she heard a voice calling her and looked up. A small, dark-haired girl in orange was running along the top of the town wall from the Laurentum Gate toward the Fountain Gate.

It was their friend Clio from Stabia. She had been trapped in Herculaneum when the volcano erupted and none of them knew whether she had survived. But now here she was in Flavia's dream, laughing as she ran. Lupus should be here, Flavia said to Nubia, still in her dream. Where is he?

Lupus hung in full sunlight, unable to brush away the flies that covered his mouth and nose. It had taken him all night to work his right arm from behind his back, but he still couldn't bring his hands to his face. Now it was after midday and he had been crying out regularly until his voice was almost gone. He was terrified that if he opened his tongueless mouth one of the big horseflies might crawl in and choke him, so he kept his lips firmly shut and tried to breathe through his nose.

It was no use crying out now, anyway. His voice had nearly gone. All he could do was curse his bad temper and pray that whoever had set the trap would check their nets soon.

Something woke Flavia and it took her a moment to realize what it was: The cart had stopped. She heard voices and rubbed her eyes. Her mouth was dry and the tops of her sandaled feet, which had been in the sunshine for the last few miles, were pink with sunburn.

"Here we are," said Feles from the front. "The great city of Rome. They won't let me in for an hour or two because I'm wheeled traffic. If you want to get to your relatives before dark you'd better continue on foot. You can hire a litter just inside the city gates."

"Thanks," said Flavia, and gratefully allowed Caudex to lift her off the back of the cart. She pulled her damp tunic away from her back, then stretched and looked around. The road was lined with tombs and umbrella pines, casting long shadows in the late afternoon sunlight. Already a line of carts sat waiting for dusk, when they would be allowed into the city. Flavia could see a white three-arched gate up ahead. Not far from it, among the other tombs along the road, was a white marble pyramid almost as high as the city walls.

Nubia came up, wearing Flavia's broad-brimmed sun hat. She was smiling.

"Did you have a nice time in the front?" asked Flavia.

Nubia nodded and took off the hat. "Feles lets me hold the reins. And he tells me the names of the mules: Pudes, Podagrosus, Barosus, and Potiscus."

"Do you know what their names mean?" asked Flavia.

"She does now,'" said Feles with a grin, and leaned against the cart. "Show us how Barosus walks."

Nubia handed Flavia the sun hat and then minced along the road in dainty little steps. Flavia laughed.

"And this is the Podagrosus," said Nubia, coming back along the hot road with a heavy, exaggerated limp. "And the Potiscus." She staggered the last few steps as if she were tipsy.

Flavia turned laughing to Feles. "Thank you very much for taking us. Here's twenty sestercii."

Feles stepped forward and took the coins. "I thought we agreed ten," he said, his catlike eyes round with surprise.

"That was before you knew Caudex was coming," said Flavia. "Fair's fair."

"Thank you, Flavia Gemina," said Feles. "I won't forget it. If you ever need a cart-driver—or help of any kind—just ask for me. I usually stay at the Owl Tavern inside the city gates, near the tomb of Cestius, that big white pyramid over there."

"Thank you," said Flavia. "Maybe we'll meet again one day." She waved and started to lead Caudex and Nubia past the tombs and waiting carts toward the three-arched gate.

"Flavia Gemina!"

Flavia turned back. "Yes?"

Feles tossed something like a ball. Flavia caught it and gasped when she saw what it was.

"An orange! But you said . . ."

"Don't worry." Feles grinned. "I'll tell them that one or two were rotten."

"Where will we sleep tonight?" asked Nubia.

"I have relatives here in Rome," said Flavia, looking around. "We haven't seen them in ages but I'm sure they wouldn't turn away their own family." She tried to make her voice sound confident. Inwardly, she was praying that they wouldn't be stranded with nowhere to stay.

Before them, a large marble fountain sputtered in the middle of a crowded square. Two main roads led from the other side of the square into Rome, no gleaming city of marble and gold, but a mass of red-roofed apartment blocks in peeling shades of putty, apricot, carrot, and mustard. Although the tall buildings threw long violet shadows across the square, the heat still muffled Rome like a woolen blanket. The stench of donkey dung, human sewage, and sweat was almost overpowering.

Flavia breathed through her mouth and looked around. To the right of the gate was a queue of litter bearers, waiting to take people into the city. On the left—up against the high city wall—were three shrines: one to Mercury, for those hoping to make their fortune; one to Venus, for those who wanted to find love; and one to Fortuna, for general good luck.

Flavia looked at the orange in her hand, a rare and valuable fruit she had never tasted. She sighed.

"Wait here for a moment," she said to Nubia and Caudex, and picked her way through donkey dung to one of the shrines. When she stood before it, she bowed her head.

"Dear Fortuna, goddess of success," she whispered, "please watch over us and help us find somewhere to sleep and not get lost or pickpocketed. And help us find our friend Jonathan." Flavia laid the precious orange in the miniature temple, among the other offerings of flowers, copper coins, and fruit.

Something tugged at the hem of her tunic. Flavia looked down and gasped.

A pile of old rags beside the shrine had lifted its head to reveal a gaunt face with terrible burns over one side.

"Please," croaked the beggar, "I lost everything when the mountain exploded. Please help . . ."

"Sorry." Flavia backed away, feeling sick. She turned and pushed through a crowd of women who had suddenly gathered to present their offerings at the shrine of Venus.

"I hope we have enough money for a litter," she muttered to Nubia and then turned to the door slave. "Caudex, you don't mind walking beside us, do you?"

Caudex shook his head. "Been sitting long enough," he said. "Good to give my legs a stretch."

"I thought you had to see the Emperor urgently." Jonathan tossed his shoulder bag onto a low cot.

"I do," said Simeon, "but I must proceed carefully."

He looked around the room and grunted. "This will do. You wait here. I'll be back as soon as I can." He went out, closing the flimsy wooden door behind him.

Jonathan stood in the middle of a small room in a cheap tenement block, a room that managed to be both dark and hot at the same time. And noisy. Although they were five floors up, Jonathan could clearly hear the people on the street far below. He went to the window and pushed at the wooden shutters.

One of the shutters was rusted into a fixed position, but after a moment's struggle the other opened with a piercing squeal of hinges. The room was flooded with the sudden hot sunlight of late afternoon.

Jonathan squinted against the light and leaned out of the window. There was a street market down below, and most stalls seemed to be selling cloth of some kind. Jonathan could hear the cries of the stallholders, the low urgent bargaining voices, the spatter of water from a fountain onto the pavement, even the clink of coins.

It was as if the stone street and brick walls amplified and focused the sound, throwing it up to where he stood. Jonathan leaned farther out, shading his eyes with his hand. He must be facing west because he could see the sun sinking above the red-tiled rooftops.

Far below he saw Simeon's head and shoulders emerge from the building and move slowly up the street. Occasionally Simeon stopped and spoke to a stallholder, then moved on. Jonathan watched his uncle until he was out of sight.

Then he closed the shutter and lay on one of the cots. It was lumpy and smelled of sour hay, but it was good to rest.

Jonathan stared up at the ceiling and cast his mind back over the day's events.

The night before, his uncle had told him something so astounding that he could still hardly believe it: His mother might still be alive! Jonathan had begged Simeon to take him to Rome. His uncle had refused, claiming it was too dangerous.

But Jonathan hadn't been able to sleep and when he heard his father and Miriam going out before dawn, he had quickly dressed and gone downstairs. Simeon had been powdering his roughly cut hair and beard with flour.

"Why are you doing that?"

"Makes my hair look gray."

"Please let me come with you," Jonathan begged. "With me along, nobody will look twice at you."

"No."

"What about my dream? Simeon. I'm meant to go with you."

His uncle hesitated.

"How old were you when you first risked your life fighting for the Zealots?" asked Jonathan.

"You could die."

"I don't care. I'll follow you whether you take me or not," said Jonathan. And he meant it.

Simeon sighed and nodded his head.

And so, pretending to be grandfather and grandson, they had found a lift to Rome on the back of a bread cart. Nobody gave them a second glance, including the soldiers guarding the gate.

Now he was in Rome. A mile, maybe two, from his mother. His heart pounded when he thought about it. Could she really be alive? Jonathan took a deep breath and closed his eyes and tried to recall the face of the woman from his dream.

Something tickled his nose and he brushed at it. Then it came again. Jonathan opened his eyes and flinched as a trickle of fine plaster dust drifted into them.

He sat up, coughing and rubbing his eyes. The drift of fine dust was coming from a crack in the ceiling above his bed. He realized he had been hearing angry voices from up there for some time now. A man and a woman. He could hear them stomping around, too.

Jonathan felt a stab of panic. He had heard stories about poorly built tenement houses and how they could collapse without warning. He was in a strange city and only one person knew exactly where he was. If the block collapsed, no one would be able to identify his body. If they even found it.

"Pull yourself together!" Jonathan muttered to himself. "Don't be such a pessimist."

Nevertheless, he went to the darkest corner of the room and crouched there. Any moment he expected the arguing couple to come crashing through the ceiling onto his bed, bringing the whole insula down around them. Pulling out his handkerchief, Jonathan pressed it to his face. He closed his eyes, inhaled its lemon fragrance, and prayed.

SCROLL IX

Nubia stretched out on the litter beside Flavia. It was like reclining on a floating couch. They had started out with the linen curtains closed, but it had been unbearably hot and the scent of cheap perfume from the previous occupant still clung to the fabric. As soon as they left the smelly area of the three-arched gate, Flavia had pulled back the curtains, and they had both sighed with relief at the cool evening breeze. Then they had settled back to watch Rome move past.

At first, the broad street they were traveling down was lined with noisy stalls. There were markets in the narrow side streets, too, though most stallholders were beginning to pack up. Some sold spices, some metal objects, some pottery. The warbling notes of a flute alerted Nubia to a side street selling nothing but musical instruments. But they were past it before she could see anything.

Presently, the stalls and shops seemed to sell higher quality goods and the pedestrians were better dressed. The stalls were replaced by shops built into the ground floor of the buildings, alternating with porches flanked by columns.

Then the litter turned so that the sun was behind them. From the angle of the couch and the puffing of the bearers' breath, Nubia could tell they were climbing a hill. Another litter passed them coming the opposite way, and Nubia turned her head in amazement. It was carried by four large Ethiopians, their skin as black as polished jet. The filmy red curtains of this litter were drawn but as it passed Nubia caught a whiff of a musky, exotic fragrance—patchouli.

There were trees here, ancient umbrella pines rising from behind walls, hinting at shaded gardens beyond. Now the shops had completely given way to porches with double doors set behind red and white columns. Sometimes the plaster was peeling, but Nubia knew this was no indication of what lay behind. Roman houses presented deceptively blank faces, with small, barred windows and heavy doors. But she knew that behind those doors were inner gardens, splashing fountains, mosaics, marble columns, and rich, elegant men and women.

It occurred to Nubia that behind each door was a different story and that there were hundreds, maybe thousands of doors in this great, strange city. She lay back on the greasy cushion, overwhelmed.

"Are you all right, Nubia?"

Nubia nodded. She wanted to tell Flavia that sometimes she felt as if everything that had happened to her in the last few months was a dream. Any moment she would wake up back in her tent in the desert, with her mother bringing her a foaming bowl of goat's milk and her little brothers squabbling on the carpets and her dog emerging from the covers, yawning and grinning. But she didn't have the words to express all that so she said simply, "Sometimes I'm feeling in a dream."

Flavia smiled and squeezed Nubia's hand. Then she turned her head away and rubbed her eye, as if to brush away a speck of dust.

The litter slowed and stopped before a porch with two simple white columns. Set back from these columns were sky-blue double doors, with big brass studs in them. They gave no hint at what lay beyond.

"Here we are," said one of the litter bearers. "The house of the senator Aulus Caecilius Cornix." He extended his hand to Flavia.

As soon as Flavia stepped onto the pavement her eye was drawn upward. Running behind the umbrella pines was a tall aqueduct, its arches red-orange in the light of the setting sun.

Flavia turned back to the litter bearer and said with all the confidence she could muster, "Please don't go until I know if they're home."

The man nodded and turned to help Nubia out of the litter.

Flavia took a deep breath, stepped forward, and banged the knocker smartly. It was made of heavy brass, shaped like a woman's hand holding an apple. Flavia heard it echo inside, and presently there was the welcome sound of shuffling footsteps. The rectangular door of the peephole slid open and dark eyes regarded her suspiciously.

"Is the Lady Cynthia Caecilia in?" said Flavia in her most imperious voice.

"Who wants her?" growled the doorkeeper.

"Flavia Gemina, daughter of Marcus Flavius Geminus, sea captain," said Flavia, and added, "her niece."

"They've gone away to Tuscany. Won't be back until the Kalends of October," he said. "Nobody told me about any guests. Come back in two weeks."

"No! Wait!" begged Flavia, her poise evaporating. "Please let us in. We've nowhere else to go and it will be dark soon!"

"Sorry." The little door of the peephole slid emphatically shut.

A terrible panic squeezed Flavia's throat and she slowly turned to face Nubia and Caudex.

The litter bearers glanced at each other and one of them stepped forward. "I'm afraid you'll have to pay us, now, miss," he said. "That'll be forty sestercii."

Flavia Gemina burst into tears.

SCROLL X

Lupus could hear a strange whimpering noise.

He opened his swollen eyelids to see what it was. But all he could see were the rough hemp ropes that formed his prison, dark against the red light of the setting sun. Presently he realized the whimpering noise was coming from his own throat.

At least the flies had left him. He opened his mouth and tried to cry out, but there was no moisture left.

He closed his eyes. Better just to die. Then his short, wretched life would finally be over. He had only two regrets. He would never know if Clio was still alive. And he would never avenge his parents' murder.

Voices were calling him. Voices from beyond. Lupus opened his eyes again.

He could just make out the god, young and beardless, with bronzed curly hair like Mercury, or the Shepherd. The young god was giving him water, pushing a skin of it through the ropes, and Lupus could feel it squirting over his swollen lips and running down his chin and then into his mouth and it was wonderful.

"Lupus! Can you hear me? How on earth did you get here? What are you playing at?" said the Shepherd, or Mercury. "You're lucky we came along. I wanted to go home. It was Lysander here who saw a deer pass this way."

Suddenly Lupus was swinging and falling and strong arms caught him and cut away the ropes and he felt cool water on his face and was finally able to fully open his eyes.

It wasn't a god. It was his tutor, Aristo, ruddy from a day in the sun, with a brace of rabbits over his shoulder, speaking Greek to his short dark friend, then smiling at the expression on Lupus's face and now laughing with his white teeth as he carried Lupus home.

Flavia sat on the sun-warmed pavement with her feet in a Roman gutter and sobbed. Nubia crouched beside her and patted her back. Caudex, still holding their bags, looked stupidly at the litter-bearer.

"Forty sestercii," repeated the bearer, with a glance at his friend.

Flavia looked up at him with red eyes. "How can it be forty sestercii?" she said through her tears. "That's twice as much as the fare from Ostia."

"She's right," said a voice behind Flavia. "You'll take ten sestercii and no more. Or I'll have to mention it to Senator Cornix." The voice was light and confident, with a Greek accent, like Aristo's.

Flavia looked over her shoulder. The sky-blue doors of the house stood open and a smiling man in a lavender tunic stepped forward. He winked at Flavia as he handed the litter bearer something. Flavia heard the clink of coins.

"Off you go now, boys," said the man in lavender, flapping his hand dismissively. The bearers glanced at each other, nodded and took their empty litter back the way they had come.

The smiling man turned to Flavia and extended a hand. "Up you get, Miss Flavia," he said. "I have to apologize for Bulbus. He's a good doorkeeper but he's as stupid as an onion. A very small onion."

Flavia laughed through her tears and took his hand, which was covered in rings. He pulled her gently to her feet.

He was not much taller than she was, slim and dark, and his bright black eyes were lined with kohl. She liked him at once.

"My name is Sisyphus." He bent his head politely. "Your uncle's secretary. I am certain that Senator Cornix and the Lady Cynthia would want to extend the hospitality of their home to a relative, even in their absence. Do please come in."

Aristo was furious.

Lupus had never seen him so angry.

"I leave them alone for a few hours and what happens?" he yelled at Miriam, who was bending over Lupus, spooning soup into his cracked mouth.

"This one runs off and gets himself caught in a boar trap, Jonathan disappears, apparently to Rome, and then Flavia and Nubia charge off after him! Do you realize Captain Geminus will hold me responsible if anything happens to them? He could take me to court, have me sent to the mines of Sicily. Or worse. Dear Apollo!"

Miriam looked up at him with tear-filled eyes.

"Oh, I'm sorry, Miriam," said Aristo. He started to reach out a hand to pat her shoulder and then let it drop to his side. Lupus knew Aristo was still in love with Miriam, even though she was betrothed to Flavia's uncle.

"I didn't mean to make you cry," said Aristo.

"It's not you," said Miriam. "It's Father. I'm worried about him."

"Don't worry," said Aristo, and this time he did touch her very briefly on the shoulder. "It's late now and the basilica will be closed, but I'll go first thing tomorrow morning and see how your father is doing." Aristo turned and looked at Lupus, and his expression softened. "And if you're feeling better tomorrow, Lupus, you can come with me."

The squalid room was filled with the deep purple gloom of dusk by the time Simeon returned. He held a sputtering oil lamp in one hand and two flat circular loaves in the other. He set the lamp on the window ledge and turned to look down at Jonathan.

"What are you doing cowering in the corner?" he asked in his deep voice.

"I'm sure that crack wasn't here when we arrived," said Jonathan. "I think the whole ceiling is going to come down on us."

Simeon looked up and studied the ceiling. "Very possibly," he said. "But if it does there's nothing we can do about it. Here. You may as well die on a full stomach." He tossed Jonathan one of the loaves. Despite himself, Jonathan grinned.

"That's better," said Simeon. He eased something off his shoulders and onto the bed. It was a long cloth case with a leather carrying strap.

"What's that?" said Jonathan, tearing a piece from his loaf as he moved out of the dark corner.

"It's a key. Our key to the Imperial Palace." Simeon undid several ties on one side of the case and pulled out a wooden instrument with four strings. It looked like a lyre, but it was longer and thinner with a bulbous sound box. "My real instrument is the psaltery," said Simeon, "but this will have to do." He gave it an experimental strum. The notes were rich and very deep.

Simeon sat on the edge of his bed and tuned the strings for a moment. "How's the bread?" he asked, as he twisted one of the wooden pegs.

"Not bad," admitted Jonathan. "It's rye and aniseed. Here." He stood and broke off a piece and handed it to his uncle and sat down again on his own bed.

Simeon grunted his thanks and ate the bread as he strummed and tuned. Finally he kicked off his sandals and settled the bulb of the instrument between the soles of his bare feet. Then he began to play.

"You're Myrtilla's daughter, is that right?"

Flavia looked up from her bowl of cold, solidified black bean soup and nodded.

"Thought so," said Sisyphus, and handed Flavia two small ceramic jars. "Sprinkle some oil and vinegar on your soup; it makes it taste much better."

Flavia did so and took another mouthful.

"I believe I met your mother once," he said. "Lady Cynthia's younger sister, the one who married a sea captain. Is that right?"

Flavia nodded.

"That's why I've never seen you here before," said Sisyphus. "My mistress Cynthia and your father fell out several years ago, didn't they?"

"Yes," said Flavia, digging her spoon in again. "I don't think my aunt likes Pater very much."

"Well," said Sisyphus, "I only met your mother the once, but I remember she was lovely. You have her nose and mouth, I think."

"Thank you," said Flavia. "And thank you for taking us in. And for the bath and the room and this soup. It's delicious."

"I told you the oil and vinegar would transform it."

Flavia and Nubia had bathed in a small cold plunge and put on fresh clothes. Now they were dining in a courtyard beneath a grape arbor. At the wooden table sat Sisyphus, Bulbus, Caudex, and a silent female slave named Niobe who was the cook and housekeeper. It was dusk, and moths fluttered round a dozen oil lamps hanging among the vine leaves.

"And you're Nubia? Flavia's slave girl?" asked Sisyphus.

Nubia nodded.

"She used to be my slave girl," said Flavia, "but last month I set her free. Now Nubia's my . . . friend."

"I utterly approve," said Sisyphus. "I hope to earn my freedom one day, too." He dabbed his mouth with a napkin and frowned at Caudex, who had already finished his soup and was wiping the clay bowl with a hunk of caraway seed bread. "Tell me, Miss Flavia, why have you made this sudden trip to Rome?"

"Well, our friend Jonathan is Jewish and his mother Susannah

died in the destruction of Jerusalem and he blames himself for some reason. But he might have found out that there are lots of Jewish women—"

"—in Titus's palace?" Sisyphus finished her sentence.

"Exactly!" cried Flavia. "I think he wants to ask them about his mother." Suddenly she frowned. "How did you know there are Jewish slaves in the palace?"

Sisyphus shrugged. "Everyone knows that Titus's palace is full of beautiful Jewish slaves. They were his gift to Berenice."

"Who?"

"My dear girl." Sisyphus put down his spoon and widened his kohl-rimmed eyes at her. "Don't tell me you've never heard of Queen Berenice?"

SCROLL XI

In a dark room in a Roman apartment block, Jonathan's uncle Simeon thumbed the deepest string of the instrument.

It was a note so deep that Jonathan did not so much hear it as feel it reverberate on the bone above his heart. Simeon pulled the string again and again until it was a beat, low and steady. Presently his other hand began to pluck the thinner strings and a melody flowed above the beat.

Then his uncle began to sing.

Once, Jonathan had felt the thick brown pelt of a mink. Simeon's voice was as soft and rich as that pelt. He sang of a weeping willow tree and a river but Jonathan was scarcely aware of the words. He closed his eyes.

Everything was strange. The sounds outside his head, the feelings inside his heart, the smells and textures of Rome. But the music carried him away from all that. He felt that if he could learn to play this strange deep lyre it would heal his pain. Or at least bring some relief.

After a time the song ended, and Jonathan opened his eyes to find his uncle looking at him with raised eyebrows.

"What's that instrument called?" said Jonathan huskily.

"It's a bass lyre. Some people call it a barbiton. This is the Syrian model. Do you like it?"

Jonathan nodded. "Will you teach me to play it?"

Simeon smiled and Jonathan realized he had never seen his uncle smile before. Some of Simeon's teeth were missing but the smile transformed his face so delightfully that Jonathan had to laugh.

Then Simeon laughed, too, and tossed him something jingly. It was a small tambourine.

"Let's see if you can keep a beat first," he said, and began his next song.

"My dears, the story of Titus and Berenice is terribly romantic." Sisyphus leaned back in his chair and took a sip of wine. A lamp hanging among the vine leaves illuminated one side of his face dramatically and made his dark eyes liquid and mysterious.

"Berenice was a beautiful Jewish queen," he began. "She met Titus in Judaea, the year before he took Jerusalem. He was a handsome commander in his prime and she a beautiful widow. They were attracted to each other like . . . those moths to the flame. They fell passionately in love. Despite the fact that she was nearly forty and he was only twenty-eight. Despite the fact that she believed in one god and he in many. Despite the fact that she was a Jewish subject and he a Roman conqueror."

Sisyphus closed his eyes.

"I saw her once here in Rome, about five years ago. She must have been at least forty-five but she was glorious! Sensuous lips, eyes like emeralds, and jet black tresses tied up with ropes of seed pearls. Her skin was silky smooth and honey-colored." He opened his eyes again. "They say she kept it soft by bathing in milk and aloes, like Cleopatra."

"Milk?" repeated Caudex thickly. He was listening as intently as the girls.

Sisyphus nodded. "What banquets they had!" he sighed. "Titus lived it up in his palace on the Palatine as if he were already emperor and Berenice his empress. Meanwhile, the real Emperor,

Vespasian, lived in a modest home in the Gardens of Sallust." He shook his head. "It couldn't last. As long as Titus was merely co-ruler with his father, the Senate could ignore his eastern lover, but as soon as Vespasian's health got worse and it looked as if Titus might become emperor . . ." Sisyphus leaned back and poured himself another glass of spiced wine.

"What?" said Flavia and Nubia together.

"I'm a Greek," said Sisyphus. "We're not afraid of strong women. But the Romans. They suspect and fear a woman with power. Especially one from the East."

He leaned forward and lowered his voice dramatically. "The Senate forced Titus to choose between the great love of his life," Sisyphus held up one cupped hand, "and their political support." He held up the other, and looked from hand to hand sadly, as if weighing two difficult choices.

"What does he choose?" asked Nubia, gripping Flavia's hand beneath the table.

"He's a Roman!" Sisyphus dropped his hands and puffed his cheeks dismissively. "Of course he chose power over love. He told her she had to leave Rome."

The girls sat back, disappointed, and Caudex made an odd clucking sound.

"But it was a difficult choice." Sisyphus nodded slowly. "They say Titus wept when he sent Berenice away, and that she wept as she went. They also say . . ." Here he leaned forward again, ". . . that he promised to recall her and make her Empress as soon as the Mule Driver died."

"Who is the Mule-Driver?" asked Nubia.

"Vespasian, of course. The old Emperor. So when Berenice left six months ago, she only took two of her many slaves, only one chest of clothing, and she only went as far as Athens. She expected to be called back very soon, you see."

"How many slaves did she have?" asked Flavia.

"Hundreds. All high-born Jewish women. They were Titus's gift to her. She also made Titus promise to be kind to all the male Jewish slaves in Rome."

Flavia frowned. "But our cart driver said that Titus put thousands of the male slaves to work on the new amphitheater."

"Pah!" Sisyphus blew out his cheeks again. "Of course they work; they're slaves. But they're well fed and their quarters quite comfortable. And do you know where Berenice's women live?"

The girls and Caudex shook their heads.

"In Nero's Golden House!"

"Oh!" breathed Flavia and Nubia and Caudex.

After a moment of reverent silence Nubia meekly asked, "What is Nero's Golden House?"

"After the great fire here fifteen years ago Nero built the most amazing palace on the ashes. It covered three hills. There were gardens, vineyards, woods, even a lake. He made Rome his villa, the Palatine Hill his atrium, and the huge lake his impluvium. The people hated him for it."

"Now I remember!" cried Flavia. "Pliny mentions the Golden House in his Natural History, doesn't he? It was made of pure gold."

"Almost," said Sisyphus. "The rooms were decorated with ivory, marble, silk, and gold." He made a dismissive gesture. "Of course, Vespasian stripped most of that away and built his new amphitheater on the site of the lake. But they say the Golden House still bears traces of its former glory, with scenes from Greek mythology painted on almost every wall, and gem-encrusted fountains and hidden corridors . . ."

"And that's where the Jewish women are?" asked Flavia.

Sisyphus nodded. "They're somewhere in it. Not sure exactly where."

"How would a person get in there?" said Flavia casually, picking a caraway seed from the table and crunching it between her teeth.

Sisyphus gave her a sharp look. "My dear, they wouldn't," he said. "Unless possibly they were one of the Emperor's slaves, and a child or a eunuch at that."

He yawned and stretched luxuriously. "Oh dear, past my bed-time. Yours too, I'd wager. I'll show you to your rooms. You girls don't mind sharing, do you?"

Flavia shook her head and Nubia said, "What is happening to Berenice now? The Mule Driver is dead, yes?"

"Yes, indeed." Sisyphus pushed back his chair and rose to his feet. "Vespasian died almost three months ago."

"And is Berenice coming back to the Titus?"

"Yes and no," said Sisyphus with a smile. "There's another story there, and a mystery as well. But I'm afraid it will have to wait until tomorrow."

Early the next morning in the port of Ostia, before dawn had tinted the sky, Lupus rose, slipped on his best sea-green tunic and made his way stiffly downstairs to the fountain. Aristo had insisted that Lupus and Miriam sleep at Flavia's house. "I don't want any more of you to go missing," he had grumbled.

Now Lupus stood beside Flavia's fountain and scrubbed his face, neck, and hands as best he could. He wet his hair and slicked it back with his fine-toothed wooden comb. Then he sat on the marble bench and waited.

Scuto and the puppies swarmed round him, wagging their tails and pawing his knees, pleading to be taken for a walk. Lupus ignored them. Even when Tigris fetched his new leather collar and dropped it hopefully on the bench, Lupus only scratched him behind the ears.

When Aristo came downstairs and saw Lupus waiting meekly for him, he smiled and gave the boy a nod. Without a word they left the house and made their way into town.

At the southern end of the forum, near the Temple of Rome and

Augustus, was the basilica, a large brick building faced with marble and surrounded by columns. The law court occupied the spacious ground floor, with offices on the first floor and prison cells at the back.

A group of men, most of them wearing togas, had already gathered outside. Because they were all waiting to see different clerks and officials, the queue moved quickly. Lupus and Aristo saw the magistrate within the hour. A slave led them up a narrow marble staircase and along a gallery overlooking the law court below.

Bato's office was the next to last on the right: a small, bright room with an arched, west-facing window. The young magistrate sat in front of this window, writing at a table covered with wax tablets and scrolls. On the floor beside him were more scrolls in baskets. Lupus noticed a small personal shrine to Hercules in one corner of the office.

"How can I help you?" Bato glanced up briefly, then continued making notes on a piece of papyrus. There was no chair for visitors. Lupus stood beside Aristo on the other side of the table.

"I am Aristo, son of Diogenes of Corinth, tutor and secretary in the house of Marcus Flavius Geminus. We've come to inquire about Captain Geminus's neighbor, a certain Mordecai ben Ezra."

Bato looked up. "Oh, yes. The Jew. I'm afraid he's being held on charges of conspiracy. The evidence indicates he was harboring a known assassin. We believe he's involved in a plot against the Emperor's life."

"Impossible," said Aristo. "He's a doctor. A healer. In fact, the Emperor recently praised him for helping the victims of Vesuvius. And Simeon couldn't be an assassin. He's Doctor ben Ezra's brother-in-law. Simeon's sister was Mordecai's wife," he explained.

Bato gave Aristo a steady look. "I know what a brother-in-law is," he said dryly. "Do you know what a sica is?"

Aristo frowned. "What?"

Bato leaned back in his chair. "I visited the doctor the day before yesterday because I was concerned about his safety. I thought he might be the assassin's target. It never occurred to me he could be the assassin's accomplice. Yesterday, however, more information came to light. It seems there are at least three assassins on their way from Corinth. One was sighted four days ago in Regium. A third was seen yesterday, coming off a ship in Puteoli. All are Jewish. All—we presume—intend to kill the Emperor. And Simeon is one of them."

Lupus and Aristo exchanged glances.

Bato tapped the end of his pen on his bottom teeth. "Tell me, Aristo son of Diogenes, have you ever heard of the Jewish revolt?"

"Of course," said Aristo. "It led to the destruction of Jerusalem."

Bato nodded. "When the Jewish revolt began fifteen years ago, a dangerous new kind of rebel came to our attention. These men were Zealots, fanatically religious, refusing to accept Roman rule. They carried curved daggers hidden in their belts or cloaks. I managed to acquire one a few years ago."

Bato rose and moved over to a small chest near his personal shrine. He lifted the lid and took out a dagger about the length of a man's hand. It was shaped like a sickle, with a razor sharp edge.

"This is a sica," he said, walking back to his desk. "Do you see how thin the blade is, and how sharp the point? No, don't touch it, boy!"

Bato raised the knife out of Lupus's reach and continued. "A swift cut at the back of the neck like this," Bato flicked the knife, "severs the spinal cord and causes instant, silent death. By the time those around the victim realize what's happened, the killer has melted into the crowd."

Aristo and Lupus exchanged glances.

"At first," said Bato, resuming his seat, "the sicarii—as these knife-men were known—only killed Jewish traitors and so-called Roman oppressors. Later, people began to seek them out and pay them to kill their personal enemies. And once they could be bought, they were no longer freedom fighters, but mere assassins." Bato's lip curled as he pronounced the final word.

"Most of them died in the destruction of Jerusalem and the siege of Masada, but a few survived. Their names are on our most-wanted list; they are enemies of the Emperor. Simeon may be the doctor's brother-in-law, but I can assure you, he is also an assassin."

SCROLL XII

Lupus and Aristo emerged from the cool interior of Ostia's basilica and stepped into the heat and noise of the central forum on a busy morning. Bato had refused to set Mordecai free on bail. He had also refused to let them see Mordecai. He had even refused to let them give Mordecai a message.

Deep in thought, Aristo automatically turned toward Green Fountain Street. Lupus brought him up short by gripping the hem of his tunic.

"What?" Aristo frowned.

Lupus tipped his head to the right and started toward the back of the basilica. Aristo sighed and followed him between the basilica's western wall and the temple of Venus, a space so narrow that sunlight never reached it.

"Ugh!" said Aristo. "It stinks here. Can't people use the public latrines?"

Lupus ignored him and continued down the passage until he reached several small square openings in the thick brick wall.

"What's this?" Aristo frowned.

Lupus pulled out his wax tablet and scribbled:

WINDOWS FOR PRISON

"Can he hear me if I talk?"

Lupus nodded.

"How do you know?"

Lupus made bug eyes at Aristo. Lupus's meaning was clear: Not now; I'll tell you later!

Aristo put his mouth to one of the gaps.

"Mordecai? Can you hear me? It's Aristo."

There was no reply.

"Mordecai?" Aristo spoke a little louder.

Suddenly they heard an accented voice. "Aristo? Is it you?"

"Yes. I'm here with Lupus. Are you all right?"

There was a moment's silence. Then: "It could be worse."

"Mordecai. We've just seen Bato. Is it possible your brother-in-law Simeon is an assassin?"

There was another long pause.

"Many years ago," came Mordecai's voice, "when Simeon was young, he joined the sicarii for a time. But he told me he'd reformed and . . . Now I may have put my family in danger. Are Miriam and Jonathan all right?"

Aristo and Lupus looked at one another. There was no point adding to Mordecai's worries.

"Yes," said Aristo. "They're worried about you, but they're both fine."

"Good." Mordecai's voice sounded tired.

"Mordecai. Is there anything we can do? Anything we can get you?"

"No. Yes! If you should see Simeon, tell him to make himself known to the authorities. That is, if he's innocent."

"I understand," said Aristo. "Anything else?"

"I could do with a wax tablet. Oh, and some of the Egyptian balm for my cellmate. He's injured."

"You're not alone?"

"No . . . there's another prisoner in here with me. He's wounded."

Lupus held up one of his wax tablets—he always carried at least two—and Aristo nodded.

"Mordecai. We're going to drop a tablet through the airhole now. Can you catch it?"

"I'm ready."

Lupus stood on tiptoe and pushed his spare tablet through the opening.

"Thank you. I've got it," Lupus heard Mordecai say.

"We'll bring you the balm as soon as we can."

"Clean strips of linen, too, if you can find them."

"Of course. Take care, Mordecai."

"Shalom, Aristo. Shalom, Lupus."

Flavia stepped out of the bedroom and stretched. Then she shivered with excitement. She was in Rome! It even felt different. Although it was not going to be as hot as the previous day, the early morning air was already warm. Humid, too. And there was a faint smell of meat roasting on charcoal: probably from the morning sacrifices.

She looked around the tiny courtyard of the children's wing. Seven bedrooms looked out onto what was little more than a light well. Splashing in the center of this paved courtyard was an orange marble fountain. A few steps took her to this fountain and she splashed her face. Nubia joined her and they both drank from cupped hands.

"Oh good! You're up," Sisyphus clapped his hands and stepped into the courtyard. He was wearing a leek-green tunic and matching leather ankle boots. "Let's go have our breakfast in the ivy pergola. It's the perfect place to plan our next move."

"You're going to help us find Jonathan?" Flavia looked at him in amazement.

"Of course." He winked at Nubia. "I haven't had this much fun in years. *Much* better than copying out the senator's speeches!"

He led them down a corridor, through a large atrium with a rainwater pool, and into the open space of a long inner garden. Although the garden was laid out with formal paths and knee-high hedges of box, it had become rather scruffy and overgrown. Flavia liked it: It looked lived in. She noticed children's toys here and there: a leather ball, a wooden horse with one broken wheel, and a reed hoop.

"How many children does my aunt have again?" she asked.

"Six last count," sighed Sisyphus, "or is it seven? I can never remember. Children don't interest me until they learn to speak intelligently. And some of them never do. I like Aulus Junior, though. He's about your age: twelve, I believe."

"I'm only just ten," admitted Flavia.

"But my dear! You're so *mature* for ten. And terribly clever."

Suddenly he stopped. "Tell me. How old do you think I am?" He struck a pose with his hands on his slim hips and turned his face to show them his profile.

Flavia and Nubia looked at each other in dismay. To Flavia he just looked old, like her father, but she knew adults always liked to be thought younger than they really were.

"Um," said Flavia, "twenty-five?"

"Miss Flavia," beamed Sisyphus, "you're my friend forever!" He linked his arms into theirs and led them on down the path to a small arbor covered with thick ivy. They had to bend to enter and it took Flavia's eyes a moment to adjust.

"Oh, it's wonderful," she exclaimed as she looked around.

Nubia nodded. "House of Green," she said.

A wooden trellis was covered in glossy ivy, so that they seemed to stand inside a miniature house with an ivy ceiling and walls. It was deliciously cool and full of a deep green light. There was just enough room for a small wrought-iron table and a stone bench on either side.

Breakfast was already laid out on the table: caraway seed bread, soft white goat's cheese, and three cups of foaming black grape juice. And arranged carefully on a small silver plate were several sections of a pulpy fruit whose color and scent Flavia recognized at once.

"Orange!" She clapped her hands and looked up at Sisyphus with delight.

"You and Lupus can't go to Rome," cried Miriam. "I'll be all alone!"

"I've asked Alma to come and stay here with you," said Aristo. "She'll bring the dogs with her."

"I want to come with you!" said Miriam, tossing her dark curls and gazing defiantly at Aristo.

She looked very beautiful, and Lupus could tell Aristo was tempted. He was about to let Aristo know it was a bad idea when the young Greek shook his head.

"What if they release your father? And what if Captain Geminus returns from his travels? Or someone brings an important message?"

"You're right," Miriam turned away. "I just feel so useless!"

"You're not useless," said Aristo. "You can help us. Rome's a big city. Flavia has probably gone to stay with her aunt, but we've no idea where Jonathan is. Just tell us anything that might help us determine where he might have gone, and why."

Miriam thought for a moment. "Ever since he smelled that lemon blossom perfume, he's been depressed about Mother's death. Flavia told me he blames himself."

"For your mother's death? But surely he was just a baby when she died."

"I know."

"Anything else that might indicate where he's gone?" asked Aristo.

"Uncle Simi left for Rome yesterday morning; so presumably they went together."

"How do you know Jonathan went to Rome?"

"His message on this wax tablet. Oh, you won't be able to read it; it's in Hebrew: 'Gone to Rome' he says, and then 'Please . . .' and the rest of the wax melted, though it's firm again now."

Lupus picked up the red and blue tablet and examined it.

Aristo shook his head. "If only we knew the rest of the message; it might help us find him."

Lupus tugged the short sleeve of Aristo's tunic.

"What, Lupus?"

TABLET IS NEW wrote Lupus on his own wax tablet.

Miriam nodded. "That's right. Gaius gave it to Jonathan for his birthday the day before yesterday."

CHEAP WAX continued Lupus.

"Probably been mixed with some lard," said Aristo. "It happens."

STYLUS PUSHED THROUGH

"What are you getting at, Lupus?"

MESSAGE UNDERNEATH?

"Of course!" Aristo snapped his fingers. "Lupus, you're brilliant!"

"What is it?" asked Miriam.

"This tablet," said Aristo, "has only been used once and the wax was very soft. See where Jonathan's stylus pushed right through to the wood?"

"Yes . . ."

"If he pushed hard to write the whole message he might have scratched the wood underneath—"

"—so his message might still be there, under the wax, which melted and then hardened again!"

Lupus nodded vigorously.

"So if we melt the wax and pour it off—" began Miriam.

Aristo finished her thought: "—We might be able to read the message hidden underneath."

SCROLL XIII

Jonathan sat in the changing rooms of the Claudian Baths in Rome and waited.

He had soaked and oiled and scraped himself and it was his turn to guard their things while his uncle bathed. Earlier, on the way to the baths, Simeon had bought them new tunics: cream linen with a black vertical stripe from each shoulder to hem. They also had the precious barbiton, and a money purse with the last of their coins.

Jonathan had put on his new tunic. He had the money purse round his neck and the barbiton safe across his lap, so he closed his eyes. Because of all the wheeled traffic, their room had been noisier throughout the night than it had been during the day. It had been so noisy that when Simeon had made some remark, although he was only a few feet away on the second bed, Jonathan hadn't been able to hear him. He had barely slept and now he was exhausted.

But he must have dozed off, because something startled him awake. A good-looking Roman stood in front of him. The man had a big head, dark blue eyes, and quizzical eyebrows. He wore a cream tunic with a black bar from shoulder to hem.

"Uncle Simeon?" Jonathan blinked sleep from his eyes.

Simeon nodded and rubbed his clean-shaven chin. "It's amazing what a good shave can do." He shouldered the barbiton and looked down at Jonathan.

"Come on," he said. "Time for us to visit the Palatine."

Lupus pushed between Aristo and Miriam, eager to see what was happening on the kitchen hearth.

"Careful, Lupus," Aristo warned. "The coals are red hot." To Miriam he said, "Just melt the wax; make sure you don't burn the wood."

"I know what I'm doing," said Miriam. "I cook every day."

Chastened, Aristo was quiet for a moment. Then he said to Miriam, "You've changed. You used to be such a shy little thing."

"I'm only shy with people I don't know." Miriam turned her head and they looked at each other for several long moments. Finally, Lupus jabbed Aristo with his elbow.

"What?" Aristo scowled down at Lupus.

Lupus pointed at the wax tablet, which was starting to smoke.

"It's burning," Aristo cried.

"No, it's not." Miriam calmly lifted the tablet off the heat with a pair of tongs and tipped it to one side. The liquid wax ran off it and was absorbed by the ashes of the hearth. Miriam replaced the tablet on the metal pan for a moment and then poured off the rest of the yellow wax.

"I can see marks," cried Aristo.

Lupus nodded enthusiastically.

"Let's take it out into the sunlight," said Miriam.

The three of them hurried out into the garden courtyard and Miriam tipped the rectangle of wood until she found the right angle of light and shadow to make the marks clear.

"Yes," she said. "I think I can read it."

"What does it say?" said Aristo.

"'Gone to Rome. Please . . . don't worry. Simeon . . . is with me. He thinks . . . Mother is . . . alive and a slave in the Golden House . . . We will try to save her.'"

Miriam's face went pale. "But Father always told us Mother was dead," she said slowly. "Simeon must have lied to Jonathan." She gripped Aristo's hand and looked up into his face. "Flavia was right: It's some kind of trap," she said. "You've got to help Jonathan!"

"Jonathan," said Simeon, "are you sure you want to do this? You don't have to come in with me. You can wait back at our rented room until I come out. *If* I come out."

They stood by a fountain in the dappled shade of the umbrella pines on the Palatine Hill. Beside them, two marble sea nymphs poured splashing water from carved shells into a granite basin.

Jonathan pulled his new cream-colored tunic away from his perspiring body. It had been a stiff climb up the Palatine Hill. He was wheezing, too.

"Just tell me again," he said.

Simeon turned his head and looked straight into Jonathan's eyes.

"I believe," he said, "that your mother is still alive and a slave in the Golden House."

Jonathan gazed back into his uncle's blue eyes and then nodded. "Then I'll come in with you."

"First you should know the full extent of my mission."

"All right." Jonathan sat on the cool granite edge of the fountain and waited.

"Three assassins," said Simeon, "have been sent from Corinth to the Palace of Titus."

"Three?" said Jonathan.

Simeon nodded and reached into his leather belt. From a hidden slit he pulled out a curved dagger.

"Three," he repeated, "and I am one of them."

SCROLL XIV

"Titus and Berenice," said Sisyphus. "were very wicked people. Before they met one another. And after."

"What were they doing?" asked Nubia. Although breakfast was over and the plates cleared away, they lingered in the green coolness of the ivy pergola.

"My dears, you don't need to know the gruesome details. Suffice it to say the people of Rome called them 'Nero and Poppea.' "

Flavia gasped.

Nubia frowned. "What is Neronpopeye?"

"Nero was an evil Emperor," said Flavia. "Poppea was his girlfriend. I know because Pater told me some of the things they did. They were horrible."

Sitting on the edge of the splashing fountain in the cool shade of the Palatine Hill, Jonathan grew pale as Simeon explained his mission.

"If they catch us before we reach the Emperor," his uncle concluded, "they may very well torture us. And afterwards they will certainly kill me, probably by crucifixion. You will most likely be enslaved. Are you still willing to come with me?"

Jonathan nodded and tried to speak, but his throat was suddenly too dry. He scooped up a handful of water from the fountain behind him and turned back in time to see Simeon toss the curved dagger underneath a myrtle bush and kick a thin layer of pine needles and dust over it.

"If they found that knife on me," explained Simeon, "I would be hanging from a cross before I could blink. Now our only weapons will be our wits." He stood up and slung the barbiton over his shoulder.

Jonathan stood too. His heart thumped and he felt sick.

"Nervous?" His uncle looked down at him.

Jonathan nodded.

"Don't worry," said Simeon. "The guards won't think it odd. Anyone about to perform for the most powerful man in the Roman Empire would be nervous."

"But my dears, let me tell you." Sisyphus leaned forward. "Since he became Emperor three months ago, the most remarkable change has come over Titus. He is completely reformed. For example. You've heard of Vesuvius?"

Flavia and Nubia glanced at each other.

"The volcano," said Flavia.

"Precisely. A terrible disaster. Thousands left ruined and homeless. And do you know what Titus did? The man we all thought would tax us to death in order to pay for his orgies?" Sisyphus slapped his thigh and sat back on the bench. "He used his own money to help the survivors!"

"Amazing," said Flavia.

"Quite," said Sisyphus. "You can be certain a man has had a real change of heart when he opens his coin purse."

"And you don't think he was just pretending to be good, to get the senators to like him?" asked Flavia.

"And for making the other people to like him?" added Nubia.

"Some people think that. But I don't. Let me tell you why I think Titus has really changed. Within a week of his father's death

Berenice hurried back from Athens, ready to be Poppea to his Nero. But do you know what happened?"

Flavia and Nubia shook their heads.

"He sent her away again! He had complete power. Could have made her his queen. Could even have kept her as his secret girlfriend. But he sent her away for the second time without even seeing her! Something has happened to him. I tell you, the man has changed."

There was an urgent snipping noise outside the ivy pergola and Flavia pushed her head out.

"Caudex!" she said. "What are you doing out there?"

"Just trimming the ivy." The big slave blushed and looked down at his feet. "And I wanted to hear the rest of the story."

Somewhere on the Palatine Hill, slaves were building an extension to the already vast palace. Jonathan could hear the faint sounds of hammers, saws, and workmen shouting. But here by the slaves' entrance it was peaceful, with only the twitter of birds and a slight breeze rustling the leaves. There was a shady porch, with cool marble benches and columns. Two soldiers stood guard, one either side of the double doors, but they kept a discreet distance.

A door slave had gone to find his superior.

"Remember," Simeon told Jonathan as they waited for the steward, "just bang the tambourine as you did last night; you'll be fine."

Jonathan nodded and told himself this was his chance to make things right.

Presently a tall man with grizzled hair appeared in the open doorway. He had a large nose and bushy eyebrows.

"Good morning." Simeon's voice was as deep and sweet as the barbiton. "We're traveling musicians. We've come to play for the Emperor."

"I'm sorry," said the steward in a well-educated voice. "We aren't allowing any strangers into the palace at the moment."

"But I thought the Emperor enjoyed listening to new music," said Simeon.

"Ordinarily, he does. But security is tight at the moment. I'm afraid it's impossible to gain access to the palace."

Simeon turned away and then back. Things were obviously not going as he'd planned.

"Is it possible to speak to someone named Agathus?" he asked.

The door-slave looked from Simeon to Jonathan and then back. "I am Agathus," he said slowly.

Simeon glanced at the soldiers standing guard nearby. Casually, with the tip of his new sandal, he traced a symbol on the dusty threshold of the porch. Before Jonathan could see it, he scuffed it out.

But Agathus had seen it. He looked up at Simeon from under his bushy eyebrows and then nodded.

"There may be a way . . ."

"So how do we know whether Jonathan has been able to get into the Golden House?" Flavia asked Sisyphus.

"I've been thinking about that." Sisyphus's dark eyes gleamed. "We have to come at this problem from a different direction."

"What do you mean?" said Flavia.

"We could waste valuable time merely trying to find out if Jonathan's been able to get in. I think we should assume he has been successful, and try to find out how we can get in to the part of the Golden House where the Jewish slaves are kept."

"So you think we should learn more about the Golden House," said Flavia slowly. "Like whether there are any secret corridors or tunnels."

"My dear, if Nero built it, there are bound to be secret corridors and tunnels. We just need to find out where they are."

SCROLL XV

"Hurry, Lupus! The cart's leaving."

Lupus looked up and down Ostia's main street. He could hear Aristo but he couldn't see him. He had just been approaching the mule driver's fountain when he heard his tutor's voice calling.

"Quickly!" cried Aristo again. "I've saved you a place."

Then Lupus saw the cart. It was already moving into the shade beneath the arch of the Roman Gate up ahead. Lupus sprinted down the Decumanus Maximus, his sandals slapping the hot white paving stones. He dodged two giggling women with papyrus parasols and a carpenter carrying planks of wood. He nearly knocked over a slave carrying a jar of urine to the fullers.

Lupus ran past the columned storefronts on his left and the long water trough on his right and charged through the Roman Gate with its laughing soldiers. He emerged into the hot sunlight again and reached out to grasp Aristo's extended hand. Then he felt himself lifted up and onto the hard, wooden bench. The other men in the cart grinned at him. The driver—who'd been going slow—gave him a wink over his shoulder before turning back to flick his whip at the mules.

"Did you give Mordecai the balm?" asked Aristo in a low voice.

Lupus nodded, then turned to watch the white marble arch of Ostia's main gate grow smaller and smaller.

He was going to see Rome at last.

■■■

In an inner room of the Imperial Palace on the Palatine Hill a dough-faced man with greasy black hair was interviewing Simeon and Jonathan.

"My name is Harmonius," he said. "Agathus has recommended you but I want to satisfy myself that you are genuine. And the only way I can do that is to audition you. We're on alert against a possible assassination attempt, but the Emperor's headaches have been particularly bad. Music is one of the few things that gives him any relief. If your music can help him, then your reward will be great." He folded his arms. "But first you must show me whether you are real musicians or merely impostors."

"There it is." Sisyphus stood beside Lady Cynthia's private litter with his hands on his hips and squinted up at an enormous structure. "The eighth wonder of the world."

Flavia and Nubia leaned out of the litter and gasped at the sight of a huge oval building, white against the turquoise sky above Rome.

"Bulbus. Caudex. Have a little rest," said Sisyphus.

The two door slaves set the litter onto the hot paving stones and helped Flavia and Nubia out.

"It's the biggest building I've ever seen," said Flavia tipping her head back and shading her eyes. "It's colossal!"

"What is it?" asked Nubia.

"It's Vespasian's new amphitheater," said Sisyphus. "When it opens in a few months there'll be gladiatorial fights, sea battles, beast hunts . . ."

"What is that twigs all over it?" asked Nubia.

"Scaffolding."

"What are they doing?" asked Flavia. "Painting it?"

Sisyphus shook his head. "They're covering it with stucco, a type of plaster. They mix it with marble dust so that it sparkles like the real thing. When they've finished," he said, "the entire amphitheater will look as if it's made of solid marble. Then they'll paint it and put statues in the niches."

Flavia glanced at Sisyphus. "There must be hundreds of slaves working on it," she said.

"Thousands, my dear. Simply thousands. And almost every one of them a captive from Judaea, brought back by our illustrious Emperor Titus."

By the end of Simeon's second song, two dozen slaves, scribes, and soldiers of the Imperial Palace had crowded into the wide doorway to listen to the music. As the last note died away, they all broke into spontaneous applause.

Harmonius passed a handkerchief across his eyes. "Extraordinary" he whispered. "I have never heard anything quite like that. Sir, you are an artist."

Simeon bowed his big head modestly, and Jonathan breathed a secret sigh of relief.

"The Emperor has an official engagement this evening," continued Harmonius, "but his younger brother Domitian is having a small dinner party here in the palace, and I'm sure he would pay you just as well. Then you can perform for the Emperor tomorrow." Harmonius stood. "Now, if you would both like to rest and prepare yourselves, I will show you to your rooms."

"Of course, there's more than one forum in Rome," said Sisyphus, helping Flavia and Nubia down from the litter a second time. "But when people say the Roman Forum, this is the one they mean."

Flavia gazed open-mouthed at the buildings towering around them. She had never seen so many columns in one place. Somehow, she'd always imagined the Roman Forum would be of pure white marble, but the roofs were red tile, almost all the statues were brightly painted, and there were dazzling touches of gold on most of the buildings.

Something else was not as she'd imagined. Apart from a few slaves going about their business and a boy driving a flock of goats between two temples, the Forum was almost deserted.

"It's so empty," she said. "I thought it would be crowded with people."

Sisyphus nodded. "It usually is," he said, "but listen."

The girls stood very still; Caudex and Bulbus, too. At first they could hear only the soft clanking of the goat bells growing fainter and fainter. Then they heard a muffled roar.

"I am hearing that earlier," said Nubia.

"It's coming from the Circus Maximus," said Sisyphus. "Just the other side of this hill, which is the Palatine, of course. The races are under way. That's the sound of a quarter of a million people cheering for their teams."

Flavia gasped. "A quarter of a million?"

Sisyphus nodded. "That's why Rome feels so empty. It's the Ludi Romani."

Nubia frowned. "What is the loo-dee ro-ma-nee?"

"A twelve-day festival to Jupiter. With chariot races every day. That's where all the Romans are. Can't stand the races myself. All that noise, dust, and heat. I much prefer a good comedy by Plautus. Or a musical recital. Now have a look behind you."

"Great Neptune's beard!" exclaimed Nubia.

Flavia shrieked: "What is THAT?"

Behind them towered an enormous gold statue of a nude man. It was almost as tall as the huge new amphitheater which stood behind it.

"It's the Sun God."

"It doesn't look like the sun god." Flavia squinted at the statue.

"You're absolutely right, my dear, it's not," he hissed. "It's actually a portrait of Nero which he erected to himself. But no Roman will give him the satisfaction of acknowledging that. Vespasian put some rays on his head and now we all call it the Sun God."

"He looks like a big pudgy bully."

"Yes," murmured Sisyphus. "It is an excellent likeness. Anyway," he continued. "Here's me." He gestured at a marble building with grayish-green columns and bronze doors. "The plans of the Golden House should be in there. They'll let me in because I work for Senator Cornix. But you won't be allowed."

"What shall we do, then?" said Flavia.

"Thought of that already," said Sisyphus. "Bulbus, take the girls to Lady Cynthia's baths. You and Caudex wait outside."

He turned to Flavia and Nubia. "You're going to enjoy one of the great pleasures of Rome," he said. "A day at the baths. Have a manicure. Or a massage. Get your hair done. Just tell them you are Lady Cynthia's niece and put it on her account. I'll see you back at the house by the eleventh hour. Hopefully with some useful information."

It was mid-afternoon of the same day when Harmonius led Jonathan and Simeon to the private dining room of the Emperor's younger brother. Domitian and his guests were just finishing their first course when Jonathan and his uncle passed between pink columns to a low platform facing the diners.

Fifteen guests reclined on five couches, eating peppered wedges of a strange orange fruit that Jonathan had never seen before. It was still early, only the ninth hour. Outside, the city of Rome was sweltering. But the summer triclinium of the Imperial Palace was a cool oasis of greens and pinks. Across the entire back wall a sheet of glassy water hissed into a trough of pink marble. Potted palms and gardenias provided color and fragrance, while six Egyptian slave girls created a breeze by waving peacock-feather fans.

Jonathan recognized Domitian at once. He was a slimmer version of his older brother, but where Titus's hair was sandy, Domitian's was brown. He was stretched out on the central couch, between a bearded man and a lovely redheaded woman.

The woman was laughing throatily at something Domitian had said. Jonathan supposed she thought him handsome. He had curly hair and large brown eyes, but Jonathan didn't like his smirk.

When Simeon had settled the barbiton between his feet, he glanced over at Harmonius, who raised his eyebrows and nodded.

Simeon bowed his head for a moment, then found the beat of his heart on the deepest string. Gradually the diners grew silent. After a moment, Jonathan echoed the beat on his tambourine, damping it somewhat to make the instrument resonate rather than jingle. Then Simeon added the melody and finally the words.

Jonathan didn't have to look at the diners to know they were moved. He felt a kind of stillness within the room. Finally, near the end of the third song, he did look up.

Some of the dinner guests were smiling and tapping the beat with their fingers. Others had closed their eyes to concentrate. But the bearded man had leaned forward and was speaking into Domitian's ear. They were both looking at Simeon, who was lost in his music.

Simeon strummed the last chord and when the applause died down, the bearded man said in a loud voice, "Well played, Simeon!"

"Thank you," said Simeon with his gap-toothed smile. And then froze.

Jonathan saw a look of panic flit across his uncle's face and he suddenly realized why. The bearded man had addressed him by name, not in Latin but in Hebrew. And Simeon had replied in the same language.

SCROLL XVI

"Oh Pollux!" Flavia heard Bulbus grumble, as they rounded a corner on their way back from the baths. "Looks like we have more visitors."

As Flavia leaned out of the litter to look, it tipped alarmingly to one side. She heard Bulbus curse as he tried to compensate for the sudden shift of weight.

"Stop the litter!" cried Flavia, and when Bulbus and Caudex obeyed, she leapt out and ran towards the two figures standing in the shade of the porch.

"Aristo! Lupus!" she cried and threw her arms around her tutor. "I'm so glad to see you!" She let Aristo go and hugged Lupus, too.

"You girls are in big trouble." Aristo tried to scowl.

Flavia tipped her head to one side. "Then why are you smiling?"

"I'm not," he grinned, and they all burst out laughing.

"Guards!" The Emperor Titus's younger brother slid off the dining couch and landed lightly on his feet.

Immediately, two soldiers stepped in from the garden and clanked to attention.

"Is your name Simeon ben Jonah?" Domitian asked Jonathan's uncle.

There was a terrible silence. The bearded dinner guest eased himself from the couch and moved to stand beside Domitian. This time he spoke not in Hebrew but in Latin. "Of course he is. I recognize him, even though he's cut his hair and shaved off his beard. Don't you know me, Simeon?"

Jonathan looked from the bearded man to his uncle. It was so quiet that he could hear the waterfall splashing into its trough at the back of the room.

"Yoseph ben Matthias," growled Simeon, and rose slowly to his feet. Jonathan stood, too.

"Precisely." The bearded man smiled around at the other diners, as if pleased that he had been recognized. "But now I am the Emperor's servant and have taken his name. You may call me Titus Flavius Josephus."

Domitian moved forward until his face was inches from Simeon's. Jonathan could smell the wine and garlic on Domitian's breath as he said, "Josephus, are you sure this man is an assassin?"

"Oh yes," said Josephus. "I'm sure. Everyone knows Simeon the Sicarius."

"Very well," said Domitian, and turned away. "Guards! Find out what they know. Then crucify this one. As for the boy . . . brand him and put him with the other Jewish slaves. And no need to bother the Emperor."

Bulbus was lighting the oil lamps when Sisyphus stepped into the dusky light of the grape arbor courtyard.

"Ah," he said with a smile. "You must be the famous Lupus. Pleased to meet you at last. Flavia and Nubia have told me all about you. And you are Aristo?"

Aristo nodded. "I hope you don't mind two more guests."

Sisyphus raised his eyebrows and said something in Greek.

Flavia's tutor laughed and replied in the same language.

"Hey!" cried Flavia. "Don't do that. I hate it when people speak a language I can't understand."

"You should understand it," said Aristo with a grin. "We've been studying Greek together for over three years."

Flavia scowled. "I know. But I don't understand when you talk fast." She turned back to the secretary. "Sisyphus," she said, "Aristo and Lupus found a message left by Jonathan. We were right. Jonathan has gone to the Golden House. But not to get information about his mother. He actually thinks she's alive! He must have gone to search for her. But Jonathan's sister Miriam is sure their mother is dead. She thinks it's some kind of trick!" Flavia stopped to take a breath.

"Why would someone go to all this trouble to trick Jonathan?" asked Sisyphus.

"Maybe Simeon is trying to trick Jonathan into helping him kill the Emperor!" said Flavia.

"That is a very real possibility," said Aristo. "Nobody expects a deadly assassin to have a boy with him."

"Did you find out how to get into the Golden House?" Flavia asked Sisyphus.

"Not yet," he said. "But I've brought some scrolls back with me. We can look at them tomorrow, as soon as it gets light."

"Good," said Flavia brightly. "Now that we're all together, I'm sure we'll rescue Jonathan from the assassin's clutches in no time at all!"

"You're lucky," said Agathus, as he and Jonathan watched a slave heat the branding iron in a brazier full of red-hot coals. "If Josephus hadn't intervened they'd be torturing you by now."

Jonathan sat shivering in his loincloth. He didn't feel lucky. They had shaved his head and searched him for lice. They had opened his mouth to examine his teeth. They had stripped him of all his possessions, including the bulla that showed he was freeborn and his ruby ring. They had even taken away his lemon-scented handkerchief. The only thing they hadn't taken was his mother's signet ring, stuck tightly on his little finger.

Agathus saw Jonathan looking at the ring. "It will come off soon enough," he said. "I imagine you'll lose quite a bit of weight in the next few days."

Jonathan stared stupidly at the steward and then looked back at the metal rod glowing red in the coals.

A slave was about to brand his left arm with the Emperor's seal. Then he would become the property of Titus Flavius Vespasianus.

"Your friend's lucky, too." said Agathus. "He'll live. If he survives the torture."

Jonathan felt ill. The bearded man named Josephus had persuaded Domitian not to kill Simeon but merely to put out his eyes and cut off his big toes. That way, Josephus had said, he'll be blind and lame and unable to hurt anyone, but we can still enjoy his beautiful music.

"Are you going to be sick again?" Agathus put his hand on Jonathan's bare shoulder.

Jonathan shook his head. "Nothing left to throw up," he muttered.

The slave was approaching with the branding iron.

Agathus squeezed Jonathan's shoulder and handed him a leather belt.

"Here, boy. Bite on this. The pain will be quite severe."

Jonathan placed the leather strap between his teeth and then took it out again.

"My handkerchief," he said, nodding toward his clothing at the end of the rough wooden bench. "Can I bite on that instead?"

"I suppose, if I fold it several times . . ." The slave stopped and waited for Agathus to bring the cloth. Jonathan inhaled its lemon fragrance to give himself courage, then clamped it between his teeth and watched the red-hot end of the branding iron move toward his shoulder.

It was not the pain that made him pass out, but the smell of burning flesh.

SCROLL XVII

"Useless!" cried Flavia, throwing down the scroll. "There's nothing here!"

It was late afternoon three days later.

Flavia and Sisyphus were in the senator's library. Scrolls lay spread across the table. Most of them contained architects' plans or accounts of Nero's reign.

Aristo and Lupus stepped wearily into the study. They had been prowling the Palatine Hill, disguised as a young patrician and his slave boy.

"Anything?" Flavia looked up at them with wet eyes.

Lupus shook his head and Aristo angrily pulled the toga from his shoulders. "I don't know how citizens can bear to wear these things," he said, tossing it onto a chair. "They're insufferably hot."

"It is one of the senator's winter togas," murmured Sisyphus, rising and going to the chair. "He's taken his light summer togas with him." He shook out the toga and carefully began to fold it.

The light dimmed momentarily as two more figures appeared in the doorway.

"Nubia, Caudex!" said Flavia. "Any luck?"

Nubia shook her head. They'd been trying to find an entrance to the part of the Golden House on the Oppian Hill.

"Big wall all round it," grumbled Caudex and wandered off toward the kitchen.

"We'll never find him!" Flavia slumped into a chair and bit her lip to keep from crying. "I'm a terrible detective."

The others sat dejectedly at the big oak table.

After a while Sisyphus spoke. "My grandmother, may Juno bless her memory, was a very wise woman. When I was a boy, I once lost a figurine that was very precious to me. I looked for it everywhere. Then one day she said, 'Sisyphus, if you stop looking for it, it might find you.' "

"Did it work?" asked Flavia.

"As a matter of fact, it did. I went to visit a friend the next day and there it was. She'd borrowed my figurine without asking."

"How does that help us?" sighed Aristo.

"Well," said Sisyphus. "Tomorrow is the last day of the Ludi Romani. I suggest we take the day off and go to the races." He shuddered dramatically. "Much as I hate them. If nothing else, it may give us a break and a fresh perspective."

Lupus whooped. Nubia sat up straight, too. She longed to see the horses run. Flavia glanced at Aristo and he gave a small nod.

"All right," sighed Flavia. "I suppose it can't hurt."

"What are you doing?" asked a little girl's voice in Aramaic.

Jonathan didn't even bother to look up. "What does it look like I'm doing?" he replied in the same language.

"It looks like you're scrubbing the latrines."

"Then I suppose that's what I'm doing." He stopped for a moment and closed his eyes. The throbbing pain in his left arm seemed to be getting worse, not better.

"You're new here, aren't you?" she asked.

"Yes," said Jonathan, trying not to retch at the smell. After a moment he said: "Where is here, anyway?"

After they branded him he had passed in and out of consciousness. He vaguely recalled being taken some distance to a cubicle just big enough for him to lie down in. For two days an enormously fat female slave had left bowls of wheat porridge outside his door. This morning she had tossed a scrub brush into his cell and told him to clean the latrines down the hall.

"You're in the Golden House," said the girl's voice.

Jonathan snorted as he scrubbed the holes cut into the long wooden bench. "Some Golden House."

"My name's Rizpah. What's yours?"

"Jonathan." Suddenly he stopped and said slowly. "The fat lady said I'm supposed to be in isolation for a week until I'm no longer unclean. She told me nobody comes here at this time of day. So what are you doing here? And how did you get in?" He turned to peer at her in the dim light of a small, high window. "You didn't come through the doorway . . ."

The little girl named Rizpah sat on the polished oak latrine behind him, between two of the holes.

Jonathan had never seen such a curious person.

She was tiny, the size of a five-year-old, but he guessed she was older, at least Lupus's age. She had perfectly straight white hair and her eyes were pink. Her skin was so fine that it was almost translucent. She wore a grubby black tunic with a white border.

"You're one of the Emperor's slaves, too," he observed.

"Of course." She swung her feet and drummed the wooden latrine with her heels. "You're handsome. I like you."

"Oh yes," said Jonathan. "Shaved head, festering brand on the arm, all covered with . . . I'm very handsome today."

"What's it like out there?" she asked presently.

"Out where?"

"Rome."

Jonathan peered at her. "You've never been outside?"

Rizpah shook her head. "I hate the sun. Anyway I like it here. It's cool and dark here. I've lived here in the Golden House all my life," she added. "Here I was born and here I'll die." She seemed to be quoting someone.

"And they call me a pessimist," muttered Jonathan. He resumed scrubbing. "Any other gems to brighten up my day?"

"I know how you could get out of here."

Slowly Jonathan put down his scrubbing brush and turned to face her. "Rizpah," he said. "I can't tell you how much that would brighten up my day."

Nubia sat forward in her seat and looked over the rail down onto the racetrack below. Then she looked across the sandy track at the strange sculptures in the central divider. She especially liked the immensely tall needle of red granite in the middle of the central island, and the seven gold dolphins at one end.

Finally she looked around at the people behind her and across the track and on either side.

"I have never seen so many peoples," she murmured.

"I know," said Flavia, and then turned to Sisyphus. "How did you get such good seats?" she asked. "Right at the front by the turning post, and in the shade?"

"They're not mine. They're the senator's," said Sisyphus. "He's got eight seats so that he can take Lady Cynthia and the howling brood. And we won't be in the shade for long, I fear. It's still early."

"Behold!" cried Nubia. "The horses."

As the first of the chariots emerged from the shaded starting gates and moved into the sunshine for their parade lap, trumpets blared and a huge roar erupted from the onlookers. Nubia covered her ears, but as the first chariot approached she forgot about the noise and leaned forward.

"Behold!" she cried. "It is the Titus!"

"Yes," shouted Sisyphus. "Today is the last day of the festival, so the Emperor himself leads the procession."

Titus rode in a golden chariot pulled by two magnificent white stallions. Dressed in purple with a gold wreath on his thinning hair, the Emperor himself held the reins. In the chariot beside him stood a rigid young man, dressed in golden armor. He seemed curiously pale and stiff to Nubia, and his eyes gazed ahead unseeing.

"Is that a statue?" shouted Flavia.

Sisyphus nodded. "It's the famous gold and ivory statue of Britannicus. He and Titus were boyhood friends, until Nero poisoned him."

Nubia leaned farther over the rail. Now the different teams were approaching.

The Blues came first, each team of four horses stepping proudly and tossing their manes as if they enjoyed the adulation of the crowd. Next came the Greens, the Reds, and finally the Whites. Each chariot was trimmed in its team colors. As the third red team came nearer, Nubia gripped the rail.

"I like those horses." Nubia brought her mouth close to Sisyphus's ear, to make herself heard above the continuing cheers of the crowd.

"Oh no, my dear." He shook his head. "Not the Red team. Only sailors and cart drivers support the Reds. You simply must support the Blues."

Nubia frowned. "But their horses are not so good."

Sisyphus scowled. "Oh, very well," he said. "If you insist." He pushed along the row and stomped up the steps toward one of the arches.

"What did you say to him?" asked Flavia. "I've never seen him get angry before."

Nubia looked worried. "I only said I am liking the Reds."

Now the third red chariot was passing directly below them. Nubia saw that its driver was an African boy not much older than she was. He wore red leather and like the other charioteers, he had tied the reins around his waist.

She tugged at Flavia's sleeve.

"Why does he tie himself to horses? What if he is being dragged?"

"I don't know," said Flavia.

"Nubia," said Aristo, raising his voice to make himself heard above the cheering. "Do you see what he's holding in his hand?"

Nubia saw the flash of bright metal. "A knife?" she said.

"Exactly. If he gets pulled out of the chariot and dragged along, he'll cut himself free."

Nubia shuddered.

Some time afterwards—she had no idea how long—the young charioteer passed again, but this time his teeth were bared in a grimace of wild joy and he was driving for all he was worth, well ahead of the eight remaining chariots. It was the final lap. A huge wave of cheering swept the circus. Nubia felt her spirit lifted up and carried along by it and then she heard herself crying at the top of her lungs: "Come on the Reds! Come on the Reds!"

She hadn't seen Sisyphus return, but she was suddenly aware that he was on his feet beside her and he was screaming for the Reds as loudly as everyone else.

"Great Juno's peacock, but it's hot! It's usually much cooler this time of year." Sisyphus fanned himself vigorously with a papyrus fan and smiled at them. "We should probably be going soon. Avoid the crush. Still, we've done very well today. We've made a tidy profit."

"What do you mean?" asked Flavia absently, cracking another pistachio nut with her teeth. She had poured the nuts onto her lap and was studying the papyrus twist they had come in: It had faint writing on it.

"We've made nearly a thousand denarii. That's more than the rent I get for these seats."

Flavia's head jerked up and she saw Lupus looking wide-eyed too.

"We've made a thousand denarii?" she said. "How?"

"Simple. I've been betting on all the horses Nubia recommended. So far she's been right about them all."

Flavia, Aristo and Lupus stared at Nubia open-mouthed. She looked equally surprised.

"My dears. Where do you think I've been rushing off to before each race? The latrines?"

Aristo said something to Sisyphus in Greek and he replied in the same language. Abruptly he stopped and looked at Flavia.

"Why are you giving me that injured look?" Sisyphus said to her. "Oh all right." He lowered his voice. "Aristo said he thought that only senators and citizens were allowed to sit in these seats. And I said he was correct, but that I have an arrangement with the steward. The senator rarely attends the races so these valuable seats would sit empty. If it weren't for us."

"So you and the steward rent them out?" whispered Aristo.

Sisyphus nodded. "We split the profits. But we only rent them to very respectable families who will behave themselves and *not lean dangerously over the parapet flicking pistachio shells onto the race track, Lupus*."

Lupus sat back and grinned at them.

Sisyphus scowled at Lupus, but there was a twinkle in his eye as he turned away. Then he gasped. "Great Juno's peacock! Is that Celer sitting over there by the Imperial Box? I thought he'd died years ago. Flavia! It's Celer!"

"Celer who?"

"Not Celer who. Who Celer. Marcus Vibius Celer. The architect. The man whose plans you've been studying for the past few days?"

"It's Celer!" cried Flavia. She leapt to her feet, scattering pistachio shells everywhere.

"Yes." Sisyphus nodded. "It's definitely time you all went home. Can you possibly take them, Aristo?"

"I think I can find the way," said the young Greek.

"It's easy," said Flavia. "We just follow the big aqueduct back up the hill."

"As for me," said Sisyphus, "I'm going to pay my compliments to old Celer over there. He owes me a few favors. And if anyone knows about secret passages or entrances to the Golden House, it will be him. After all, he built it."

SCROLL XVIII

Jonathan was moving through blackness with nothing to guide him but the hand of a small girl.

"How do you know where you're going?" Jonathan said into the void. "And how did you find these tunnels?" He heard his voice echoing back from the moist plaster walls.

"I told you," came Rizpah's voice. "I've lived here all my life. There are tunnels everywhere. Some of them are blocked up now but most aren't. Mother said the Beast built them."

"The Beast?" Jonathan's Aramaic was a bit rusty. His father always insisted on them speaking Hebrew at home.

"The Beast. Neeron Kesar."

"Oh. You mean Nero."

"That's what I said."

"Rizpah. Is your mother here?"

"Of course."

"Could I see her?"

She must have stopped, because he bumped into her.

"Sorry, Rizpah."

"Jonathan." He could tell from her voice that she was trying to be patient with him. "Do you want me to get you out, or do you want to meet my mother?"

"Are there other women with your mother?"

"Of course. They weave wool in the octagonal room."

"Rizpah," he said into the void. "I want more than anything to get out of here. But I came to Rome to find my mother. Her name is Susannah. Is there a woman named Susannah ben Jonah with the others?"

There was such a long pause that if he hadn't been holding her moist little hand he would have thought himself alone.

Finally Rizpah's voice came out of the blackness. "There is a woman called Susannah the Beautiful. But she is not with the others. She weaves on her own." He felt her hand clench in his as she added, "They call her the Traitor."

As Flavia and her friends emerged from the shaded exit of the Circus Maximus and stepped into the blistering heat of a Roman afternoon, they scattered a group of feral cats that had been scavenging a discarded lunch. Most of the cats fled, but one of them—a tortoiseshell—looked up at them with round eyes.

"Great Juno's peacock!" Flavia exclaimed. "Feles!"

"What?" said Aristo. Lupus echoed the question with his bug-eyed look.

"Feles . . . driver of cart?" said Nubia.

"Yes! I'm so stupid!" Flavia hit her forehead with the palm of her hand. "That cat reminded me of him. Feles told us his girlfriend is a slave in the Imperial Palace on the Palatine Hill. She might know how to get in. I should have thought of this days ago."

"Never mind, you've thought of it now," said Aristo. "How do we find her?"

"We'll have to ask Feles. He stays at the Owl Tavern just inside the gate."

"Which gate?"

"The gate with three arches by the big white pyramid."

"That's the Ostia Gate," said Aristo. "It's not far."

Lupus held up his wax tablet:

WHAT ARE WE WAITING FOR?

"Rizpah," whispered Jonathan. "I think I can see light up ahead."

"It's the octagonal room," came Rizpah's voice. "That's where my mother is."

They were crawling along a low tunnel. As they moved forward, the blackness brightened to gray and then gold. Presently they reached the square end of the tunnel.

Jonathan peered out, squinting as his eyes adjusted to the light. He found he was looking down onto a vast octagonal room full of women weaving at looms. The weavers filled the space below him and the five large alcoves around it.

Above the courtyard rose a vast domed roof, covered with rough concrete, lit golden by the light pouring through a large circular skylight. The beam of sunshine illuminated the wool dust suspended in the air, and to Jonathan it looked like a fat gold column that had tipped to one side.

From somewhere to his left came the sound of falling water.

"What is this place?" whispered Jonathan.

"I think this used to be the Beast's dining room," said Rizpah. "My mother calls it the Pavilion, because when she first came there was cloth inside the dome and it looked like a big tent. I don't remember. I wasn't born then." She pointed. "That's my mother over there, the one with the fluffy brown hair. See? The one working on the red and blue carpet. Her name is Rachel."

All the women wore black robes, as if they were in mourning. A few had pulled black scarves over their hair but most had left their heads uncovered.

"And Susannah the Beautiful?" asked Jonathan.

Rizpah looked at him with her pink eyes. "She isn't here."

"I know. But can you take me to her?"

Rizpah nodded. "Yes. Do you want to see her now or talk to my mother first?"

"I'd like to see her now." Jonathan's heart was pounding.

"Then we have to go farther on," said Rizpah. "She's in a special place we call the cave of the Cyclops."

Flavia and her friends found the Owl Tavern between two lofty tenement blocks on a street so narrow that it probably saw the sun only at midday.

"I don't like it here," said Aristo, pulling aside the curtain of the litter so that Flavia, Nubia, and Lupus could climb out.

The smell of sour cabbage mingled with the sickly-sweet odor of human sewage. Flavia squealed as something dripped on her shoulder, but it was only some wet laundry hung overhead.

"At least we have Bulbus and Caudex to protect us," she said, trying to breathe through her mouth.

Aristo looked around. "I still don't like it. Let's find this Feles quickly and get out."

"Yes," lisped the innkeeper a few minutes later. He was a hideously ugly man with a harelip and a lazy eye. "Feles is here. Only he's not here. He took his girl to the races." The innkeeper smiled and his lip split even farther to revealed orange teeth, the result of pink wine stains on yellowing enamel.

"We've just come from there," said Flavia, looking him steadily in his one good eye so that she wouldn't have to look at the rest of his face. "The races should have finished by now."

"Then he'll probably be back any moment. Shall I get you a jug of wine while you wait?"

"No," said Aristo hastily. "We must get back. But could you give Feles a message? Ask him to go to the house of Senator Cornix on the Caelian Hill. It's the house with the blue doors at the foot of the aqueduct." He flipped the innkeeper a copper coin.

The others turned to go, but Flavia stayed a moment longer and forced herself to look back at the innkeeper.

"Please tell Feles," she said politely, "that Flavia Gemina needs his help."

"Be careful, Jonathan," said Rizpah, "it's slippery here." The space they were moving through now was not so much a tunnel as a channel. Water ran between them along a shallow concrete trough. On either side of the running water was a space just big enough for them to crawl on their bellies. Rizpah wormed her way expertly along the right-hand bank of the channel, Jonathan moved more laboriously on the left. They were heading toward a chink of light the shape of an eye.

Presently, the chink grew bigger and brighter and Jonathan could hear the sound of foaming water. The brand on his left arm throbbed and his elbows were raw from pulling himself forward along the rough concrete, but he ground his teeth against the pain and moved steadily on.

Abruptly the water fell away, splashing onto sculpted rocks and into a pool.

As his eyes adjusted, Jonathan found himself looking into a large vaulted room designed to resemble a cave. The floor was polished black marble and the walls encrusted with shells, pumice, and imitation pearls. Stalactites of sculpted plaster hung from the ceiling.

At the far end of this long, manmade cave he could see columns silhouetted against the bright inner garden beyond. The soft greenish-yellow light that filtered in from the courtyard was reflected off the pool and formed wobbling rings of light on the stalactites.

At the brighter end of this bizarre room a solitary woman sat before a loom. Jonathan could not see her face, because she had just turned her head toward the garden, but he saw that she wore the black robes marking her out as a slave of Titus. Her head was uncovered, and her black hair was as smooth as silk.

Presently, the woman turned her head back toward the loom. When Jonathan saw her profile, his heart pounded so hard he thought he might die. She was beautiful, like Miriam, with the same dark eyebrows, straight nose, and full lips.

He knew it was his mother.

As he watched, a man appeared in the garden, his stocky body silhouetted as he passed through the columns and approached the woman. Her head turned again; she rose and stood with her back to Jonathan.

The man walked to the woman and took her hands in his. She was as tall as he, and he looked directly into her face. The man shook his head and put his arms around the woman, patting her back as if to comfort her.

He was powerfully built, with a square head and sandy hair. And although he was not wearing his purple toga or his golden wreath, Jonathan knew the man embracing his mother was the Emperor Titus.

SCROLL XIX

When Flavia and the others returned from the Owl Tavern, they found Sisyphus waiting for them in the atrium.

"Where have you been?" His eyes were shining.

"To an inn near the big pyramid by the Ostia Gate," said Flavia. "Our cart driver's girlfriend is a slave at the Imperial Palace and we were trying to find him."

"Any luck?" Sisyphus giggled.

"No," said Aristo, "but by the sound of it *you* have."

"Yes, yes, yes!" Sisyphus clapped his hands together. "Miss Flavia. Do you remember the plans of the Golden House we pored over? How some of the walls were shown with double lines?"

"Yes," said Flavia. "A black line next to a red line. We thought that meant the walls were extra strong."

"No, no, no! Celer told me the red lines mark the location of secret tunnels!"

"But that means," said Flavia, her eyes wide, "that there are dozens of tunnels all over the Golden House!"

"And remember we puzzled over one or two red lines wandering off into the gardens? Those must be the places where the tunnels lead from the inside out!"

"Or," said Flavia, "from the outside in!"

■■■

"Why didn't you tell me the Emperor and my mother were lovers?" said Jonathan to Rizpah.

They had wriggled back to one of Rizpah's secret dens, between the octagonal room and the cave of the Cyclops.

"They aren't lovers," she said. "All the women think they are but I know they're not."

"It looked that way to me."

"They're just friends. He visits her and talks to her every day but he doesn't spend the nights. Sometimes I hide here and listen to them talking."

"How long has this been going on?"

"Since Berenice left. Five or six months."

Jonathan groaned and leaned back against the damp wall. All these years, he had believed his mother was dead. But she had been right here in Rome, less than fifteen miles from Ostia. And Titus, the greatest enemy of the Jews, had been with her daily for half a year: talking to her, holding her hand, gazing into her eyes.

Jonathan felt sick. He was finding it hard to breathe. He closed his eyes, calling to mind the day he had first met Titus on the beach south of Stabia, less than a month ago. On that occasion, Titus had hurried back to Rome as fast as he could. To be with her?

Jonathan opened his eyes.

Everything his uncle Simeon had told him made sense now.

Leaning against the opposite wall, Rizpah was watching him steadily. Light filtered in from somewhere above. He could see a pile of rags beside her, presumably her bed. Near it were a few flat loaves of black bread and a ceramic jug.

"Rizpah," he said, still trying to breathe. "There's something I've got to tell you. I have to tell someone and I don't know who else to tell."

"Then tell me," she said. "But first, drink this." She held out the clay jug.

He nodded and drank straight from the jug, long and deep, and came up gasping.

"And eat this." Rizpah tore a piece of bread from the dark loaf and handed it to him.

"I can't. If I eat it I'll just throw it up."

"No you won't." Her tone was surprisingly firm. She pushed it into his hand. "Eat it," she said.

The bread was leathery but tasted of honey. It was good.

"And you need one more thing," she said.

"What?"'

"This." Rizpah reached into the pile of rags and extracted a tiny ball of gray fluff. She placed it in Jonathan's lap. It was warm and it mewed.

"A kitten," said Jonathan, and held up the tiny creature. The mother cat lifted her head from the bedding and studied Jonathan. After a moment she lowered her head again to attend to the rest of her litter.

Jonathan cupped the tiny creature in his hands and held it close to his filthy black tunic. As the kitten felt the warmth of his body and the beating of his heart it began to purr.

"It's impossible," whispered Jonathan, shaking his head.

"What's impossible."

"That something this tiny could make a noise so loud."

And then, at last, he wept.

"Yes, I used to be a slave in the Golden House," said Feles's girlfriend, Huldah. "But Queen Berenice didn't like me, so she sent me away to the Imperial Palace on the Palatine Hill. I much prefer being a slave there. I get one day a week off and I can meet Feles when I go to the markets."

Feles and Huldah had arrived at the fifth hour after noon, just as dinner was being served.

Flavia frowned. "But isn't the palace on the Palatine part of the

Golden House? I mean, the plans showed . . . isn't the Golden House spread over three hills?"

Huldah shrugged and tore at her chicken leg with small white teeth. She was extremely pretty, with a curvaceous figure and slanting black eyes. "Not sure," she said with her mouth full. "All I know is that we call it the Golden House. It's not on the Palatine. It's part of the Esquiline Hill. The one the other side of the new amphitheater. We call it the Oppian."

"The banqueting pavilion!" cried Sisyphus. "Celer told me. It was an enormous complex full of nothing but dining rooms for Nero to entertain his guests and show off his works of art."

Aristo nodded. "So who exactly lives in the Golden House on the Oppian Hill?"

"It was Berenice's quarters," said Huldah. "Just far enough from the official palace to be discreet, but close enough for Titus to visit her. Or vice versa. After the destruction of Jerusalem she asked Titus to spare all the noblewomen of Jerusalem. So he did. We were his gift to her."

Huldah sucked the last shreds of meat from her chicken leg and took a handful of olives.

"Berenice looked after us," she said, refilling her wine cup. "We wove beautiful carpets and told each other stories and sometimes we had music. Some of the women even have their children with them. They have their own slave school. And Titus let us observe the Sabbath and keep the feasts." She spat an olive stone onto her plate and grinned. "We lacked only one thing." Here she slipped her arm round Feles and gave him a squeeze: "Men."

"Do you ever go back there?" asked Flavia.

Huldah snorted. "You'll never get me back there. Besides, once you're out of the Golden House, you can never go back. You're unclean, or something."

"So nobody goes there?"

"Nobody but Titus and female musicians. He gets bad headaches and music is the one thing that helps. Oh, and sometimes we had child entertainers. But no men. We were like the Emperor's harem, except Berenice was the only one he ever visited." She pouted.

"Why did Berenice send you away?" asked Sisyphus, then added in a conspiratorial tone. "Or shouldn't I ask?"

Huldah looked up at him from under thick eyelashes and popped another olive in her mouth. Then she grinned. "Why do you think? Berenice was jealous of me. I was fifteen, she was almost fifty. She saw Titus looking at me once. Then, ecce!" Huldah spat the olive stone across the courtyard. "I was out of there like a bolt from a ballista."

Lupus guffawed.

Feles looked at Huldah. "You are beautiful enough to be an empress, you know."

Huldah shrieked and elbowed him in the ribs. "Oh you!" She took a long drink of wine and as she wiped her mouth with the back of her hand the copper bangles on her arm jingled. "I just love my little tomcat." She squeezed Feles round the waist again and nibbled his earlobe. "Couldn't do without him now."

Flavia looked around the table. Aristo, Caudex, and Bulbus had glazed looks on their faces. Even Lupus was staring open-mouthed at Huldah. Sisyphus winked at Flavia and she cleared her throat.

"Huldah," she said, "was there a woman among the slaves from Jerusalem named Susannah? Susannah ben Jonah? Something like that?"

Huldah scowled. "There are two or three women named Susannah," she said. "And one they call Susannah the Beautiful. But she's much older than I am. And I don't think she's so very beautiful." Huldah tossed her hair and turned to Feles. "Let's go, tomcat," she said. "I'll get into trouble if I'm not back soon."

■■■

Somewhere in a secret room of the Golden House, Jonathan dried his eyes. The tears had brought a kind of release. His mother was the Emperor's slave, but at least she was alive. And as long as she was alive, there was hope that he could save her and somehow bring her home.

He cradled the kitten in his left arm and felt its tiny, needlelike claws dig into the crook of his elbow. The pain was nothing compared to the throbbing of his branded shoulder. With his right hand, he slowly reached for another piece of bread.

"You were going to tell me something important," said Rizpah.

Jonathan nodded and bit into the bread. "Do you know Queen Berenice?"

Rizpah nodded. "I've known her all my life, till she went away six months ago."

"Is she nice?"

Rizpah shrugged. "She was kind to us. But all she talked about was Titus and how one day she would be Empress. When Vespasian died and Titus became Emperor a few months ago she came back. But he wouldn't even see her. He sent her away for the second time in half a year."

"Yes," said Jonathan slowly, thinking about what Simeon had told him, "that makes sense. Last month—that must have been after Titus sent her away the second time—Berenice went to Corinth. That's a seaside town in Greece where there are lots of Jewish slaves. She visited the slaves and pretended to be buying some as bodyguards for the Emperor. But really she was looking for assassins to send back here to Rome."

"To kill Titus?" Rizpah frowned. "But she loves him. Even though he keeps sending her away. Besides, if she killed him she'd never be Empress."

"Not to kill the Emperor," said Jonathan. "Berenice hired three assassins to kill the woman she thinks he's fallen in love with."

Rizpah's pale eyes widened. "Your mother!" she breathed.

Jonathan nodded. "My uncle wouldn't tell me all the details, but now I've seen for myself. Berenice must think that if my mother, Susannah, died, Titus would be sad for a while, but then he would send for her and things would be the way they were again. He'd make her his Empress. That's why she hired the assassins to kill my mother. What Berenice didn't know was that one of the assassins she interviewed was my mother's brother Simeon."

"God must be looking after her," said Rizpah.

"Yes. My uncle thought that, too. When Berenice asked him to go to Rome to kill a Jewish woman called Susannah the Beautiful, he suspected it might be his sister. So he accepted the job, risked his life, and came to warn his sister, if it was really her. He knows what the other two assassins look like. They each took different routes and I think my uncle got here first."

"Why did your uncle disguise himself as a musician? Why didn't he just warn Titus about the other assassins?"

"Berenice told my uncle and the other two assassins that she had an agent in the palace—someone high up—but she wouldn't tell them who. She said her agent would be watching them and would kill them if they tried to warn Titus. And they would be paid only after they had done the job."

Rizpah nodded and Jonathan continued, "My uncle was trying to reach the Emperor directly without letting anyone else know who he was. But then Domitian caught us . . ." Jonathan stopped stroking the kitten. "By now they will have cut off Simeon's big toes, so that he can't walk, and blinded him, so that he can't even point out the other assassins." Jonathan hung his head. "And it's all my fault. All of it."

SCROLL XX

"Why is everything your fault?" Rizpah asked Jonathan.

Jonathan wiped his eyes with the back of his hand. "We were living in Jerusalem when I was born. But my father knew of a prophetic warning that Jerusalem would fall. 'When you see Jerusalem being surrounded by armies, you will know that its desolation is near.' My father always quotes that," added Jonathan. "He took Miriam and me to a village called Pella where there were other . . . where he believed we would be safe. But my mother refused to go with us."

"Why?" asked Rizpah.

"I'm not sure. All I know is that it had something to do with me."

"But weren't you just a baby?"

Jonathan nodded. "I was one and a half."

"Then how could it have been your fault?"

"I don't know. But last week I heard my uncle tell my father that it wasn't his fault. He said, 'She'd made up her mind to stay because of Jonathan.' I'm sure it was my mother they were talking about, because my father was crying."

Jonathan felt Rizpah watching him as he stroked the kitten.

"And you're sure your uncle meant you?" she asked softly.

"Who else would he be talking about?" said Jonathan. "Besides, I've always known it was my fault."

"How?"

"I just know."

"And that's why you risked your life to save her," said Rizpah.

Jonathan nodded. "I have to make it right," he said. "I have to find some way to rescue her and bring her home."

"Here!" said Flavia, punching the scroll with her forefinger. "This entrance by the lake leads to the big octagonal room. That's how we'll get in."

"Oooh, it's exciting, isn't it?" said Sisyphus.

Flavia looked up at him.

"Sisyphus. You heard what Huldah said: Only women and children can go into the Golden House."

"No!" The scrolls on the table jumped as Aristo slammed his fist down. "You can't possibly imagine I'm going to let you go down some tunnel all by yourselves? Absolutely not."

"But Jonathan is our friend. We have to do something!"

"Flavia." Aristo passed a hand across his face. "I care about Jonathan, too. But I cannot allow you to go in there on your own."

"We probably won't even be able to get into the gardens," said Flavia. "But couldn't we just look? I promise we won't do anything unless you give permission. Please, Aristo?"

"Jonathan," said Rizpah. "Was your uncle the only one who knew what the other assassins looked like?"

It was dark in Rizpah's den, for night had fallen. There was just room for the two of them on the pile of rags, with the kittens in between.

"Yes," said Jonathan. "But he described them to me. One is called Eliezar. My uncle said he's a big man with red hair and beard and a scar on his forehead. The other one is called Pinchas. He's small and dark and one of his eyes is half brown and half blue. It's a good thing men can't get in the Golden House," he added.

There was a pause in which he could only hear the kitten purring. Then Rizpah said, "That's not completely true . . ."

Lupus, Flavia, and Nubia stood at the three points of an imaginary triangle and tossed a leather ball slowly back and forth. Aristo and Sisyphus stood nearby chatting quietly and staring out at the new amphitheater. Lupus knew that to play trigon properly they should have been throwing the ball very rapidly as hard as they could. However, their focus was not on the game but on the gardens behind the thick wall.

It was early morning of the next day and they stood on the shaded slopes of the Oppian Hill. To their left and below them was the new amphitheater, so close that occasionally Lupus could hear the voices of the slaves calling to each other on the scaffolding. To their right, rising up behind the other side of the wall, were tall umbrella pines, cypress, and cedars: the gardens of the Golden House. They had found a place where the earth was highest against the wall, and it was almost possible for Aristo to see over it.

When they were close enough to the wall to see the cracks in the yellow plaster, Flavia nodded at Lupus and he deliberately threw the ball over the wall.

"Oh dear," said Flavia loudly, in case any guards were nearby. "Our ball has gone over the wall. What shall we do? Slaves! Come here and help us!"

Aristo and Sisyphus glanced at each other and grinned.

"What do you require, mistress?" asked Sisyphus in a mock humble tone.

"Lift up my little brother so he can see where our ball went," Flavia commanded.

Lupus felt himself lifted up by the two Greeks, each of whom had grasped a leg. As his head rose above the top of the wall, he found himself staring straight into stern eyes beneath a polished helmet. A woman guard!

"Aaah!" Lupus yelled and his arms flailed.

Startled, Flavia and Nubia squealed. Aristo and Sisyphus cursed as they tried to keep hold of Lupus. They managed not to drop him, but the three of them collapsed in a heap on the ground.

"Oh Pollux!" Sisyphus brushed himself off. "Pine needles and dust all over my best mauve tunic!"

Lupus's brief glimpse had shown him that the gardens were terraced; the ground level was much higher on the other side of the wall. He, Aristo, and Sisyphus scrambled to their feet and looked up at the face glowering down at them.

"What do you think you're doing?" The guard's voice was stern.

"Please, miss." Flavia used her little girl voice. "We were just playing and our ball went over."

"Do you behold it?" Nubia asked.

Flavia added, "Our slaves here were just lifting up my little brother so he could see where it went. It's his favorite toy. Isn't it, Lupus?" She looked pointedly at him.

Lupus employed one of his least favorite tactics. He burst into babyish tears.

"Oh dear! Don't cry, little boy! I didn't mean to frighten you." The woman's head disappeared and a moment later she was back. The ball dropped onto the ground beside them. "There's your ball. Now, you mustn't play here again. Do you know why?"

Lupus and the others shook their heads.

The guard attempted a friendly expression. "Yesterday we caught a bad man trying to climb over this wall," she said. "A huge red-haired Jew with a very sharp knife. We think he was trying to kill the Emperor. So we're guarding this whole area very carefully. Now do you understand why you mustn't play here?"

Lupus sniffed and wiped his nose on the back of his finger. The two girls nodded meekly.

"We won't ever play here again," lisped Flavia, and then asked in a tiny voice, "what happened to the bad man?"

"Oh, he was a very bad man," said the guard. "They crucified him this morning at dawn."

SCROLL XXI

The moment Jonathan woke up, his stomach clenched as he remembered the momentous thing he had discovered. His mother was alive.

He lay curled up on Rizpah's pile of rags and gazed up at the dim light filtering in from above. Next to him the kittens mewed. They were looking for their mother.

He could smell the salty dampness of the walls and the faintly sweet smell of cat's milk.

The mother cat stalked into the den. Rizpah followed her in on hands and knees.

"Good afternoon, Jonathan. You slept a long time."

He yawned and winced as he used his left arm to push himself to a sitting position.

Rizpah handed him the jug and he brought it to his lips. It was buttermilk, thick and tart and delicious. It made him think of home. Of Ostia. He wondered what his father and Miriam and his friends were doing there now.

He handed Rizpah the jug, but she shook her head. "I've had breakfast. Ages ago." She sat cross-legged, stroking the smallest kitten, a purring bit of black fluff.

Jonathan drank again and finally put down the empty jug. Rizpah ran her finger inside the neck of the jug and let her kitten lick the buttermilk off.

Jonathan gently took the gray kitten, which he had named Odysseus, and followed Rizpah's example. He laughed as he felt the kitten's warm tongue wetly sandpapering his finger.

"Rizpah," he said after a moment. "Don't you have any slave duties?"

"No. The guards aren't even sure I'm still here. My mother and the other women know I'm here but they'd never give me away. I can go places nobody else can and so I tell them what's happening. The guards used to look for me but they never found me." She wiped her finger in the jug again and then added, "They've been looking for you, too. But now they've given up." She giggled. "The women who run the slave school think you've fallen down the latrine pit."

"There are women teachers?" said Jonathan, amazed. And when Rizpah nodded, he murmured. "It's strange that there are no men here."

"It was Berenice's idea. She didn't want any men around. After what happened."

"What do you mean?"

"I mean what happened after the Romans finally took the city."

"I still don't understand."

"Jonathan," said Rizpah. "I am eight years old. My mother is Rachel. I don't know who my father is. Neither does she. There are twenty-three of us here at the Golden House, all eight years old, all born in June."

Jonathan frowned.

"All born in June," repeated Rizpah, and added, "Nine months after the legions entered the city."

"Oh!" said Jonathan, and then: "I'm sorry."

"Don't be," said Rizpah matter-of-factly, and kissed her kitten on the nose. "Here I was born and here I'll die."

"Rizpah," said Jonathan. "I need to see my mother. Now that they've captured my uncle, I'm the only one who knows about the assassins Berenice sent. I have to warn my mother. Is there another way to her room, apart from the fountain tunnel?"

Rizpah nodded. "I've been waiting for you to ask me. I'll take you now."

At the slave entrance of the Imperial Palace on the Palatine Hill stood a quintet of traveling musicians, three of whom were children. On their heads were flowered garlands entwined with ribbons. Each of the musicians wore a different colored tunic. The flautist was a dark-skinned girl in yellow, the drummer a younger boy in green, and the girl with the tambourine wore blue. A handsome, curly-haired Greek in a red tunic played the lyre and a slender, dark-haired man in mauve shook a gourd full of lentils.

They had just finished a short musical piece and now this colorful quintet gazed hopefully at a grizzled slave and a dough-faced man.

The two men looked at one another, nodded, and beckoned the musicians inside.

Jonathan was following Rizpah through one of the tunnels back to the octagonal room when she jumped down into an immensely long, high corridor.

"This is a different way," said Rizpah. "I don't like it as much. It's too bright. But it's faster." The dim vaulted corridor was covered with plaster and all the walls were painted with delicate frescos in purple, azure, and cinnabar red. Some of the fresco panels on the wall of the corridor were the same designs as the carpets the slave women had been weaving. Even though the light was muted, Rizpah shaded her eyes against it.

"They call this the cryptoporticus. That means 'secret corridor,' but it really isn't secret," she said. "I don't think we'll meet anyone, but if we do, let me do the talking."

■■■

"I'm afraid you men will have to wait here on the Palatine," Harmonius said to Aristo and Sisyphus. "The Emperor wants music at the Golden House immediately, but no men are allowed there. Only women and children. Don't worry," he said, as the Greeks started to protest. "You'll all be paid handsomely and you'll find your quarters most comfortable. When the children have finished they'll be escorted back here. Then you'll perform for Domitian."

"But who will look after them while they perform at the Golden House?" said Aristo.

"My dear fellow, they're only going over to the Oppian Hill and they'll be under the Emperor's protection. What harm could possibly come to them?"

"He's still with her," hissed Jonathan. "Why doesn't he go away? Doesn't he have an empire to run?"

"I don't know," Rizpah answered. "Something must have happened. He looks upset. He usually only visits her first thing in the morning or last thing before dusk."

Jonathan and Rizpah had approached the cve of the Cyclops from ground level—through the garden—and had found a hiding place behind a glossy shrub with bright orange berries.

Jonathan watched his mother and the Emperor. They sat facing each other on elegant folding armchairs in the shade of the peristyle, halfway between the bright garden and the dim cave.

Jonathan strained to hear what they were saying but the sound of a fountain splashing in the garden made it impossible to distinguish anything apart from his mother's coughs.

"She's not well," he muttered. "She's coughing. If my father were here he would prescribe mallow boiled in milk. Or a tincture of ryegrass."

Rizpah touched his arm reassuringly. "All the weavers cough," she said. "My mother says it comes from breathing the wool dust. Don't worry."

"And now she's crying. Look! Titus has made her cry!"

"Shhh!" said Rizpah, "If they hear you, they'll take you away and you'll never get a chance to warn her. Oh look! Here comes Benjamin."

A dark-haired slave-boy approached the cave of the Cyclops and waited discreetly outside. He was about Rizpah's age, and Jonathan could see by his shiny hair and spotless black tunic that he was not on latrine duty.

Presently Titus glanced over at him. The young slave bowed his head respectfully and said something. Jonathan caught the word "musicians."

Titus nodded, said something to Susannah, and rose to his feet. He and the boy disappeared in the direction of the octagonal room.

Jonathan's mother watched them go, then she slowly stood and closed her eyes for a long moment. Presently she opened them again and moved into the sunlit garden, toward the very bush that hid Jonathan and Rizpah.

SCROLL XXII

"Great Juno's peacock!" exclaimed Flavia. "Look at that." She parted the filmy purple curtain at the front of the Imperial litter and the three of them rolled over onto their stomachs, gazing out in wonder.

Above and before them lay an immensely long palace built into a green wooded hill. It was fronted with a row of dazzling golden columns that blazed in the late afternoon sunlight.

"There must be a thousand of those columns," breathed Flavia. "Do you think they're solid gold?"

Lupus shook his head and made a painting motion.

"Just gilded? Still, that's a lot of gold paint . . . Now we know why they call it the Golden House."

Above the yellow-tiled roof of this dazzling complex, on the crest of the hill, she could see fountains, a portico of smaller white columns and seven palm trees planted in a circle.

The bearers puffed as they carried the litter up marble steps between green terraces.

"Great Juno's peacock!" cried Flavia again. "A peacock."

"Behold! Its tail is spreading," whispered Nubia. Flavia could tell from Lupus's round eyes that he had never seen a peacock before. Somewhere behind the fragrant shrubs which lined the stairway, another peacock uttered its haunting cry.

Now the litter had reached the top of the marble steps, and the highest terrace came into view. Several long reflecting pools lay at the foot of the long portico, doubling the golden columns. A dozen exotic wading birds with curved beaks and orange-pink feathers stood in the pools among clumps of papyrus and floating water lilies.

Nubia uttered a word Flavia didn't understand.

"What?"

"Those birds are from my country," said Nubia.

The four burly slaves carried the litter between two of the reflecting pools, then set it down beneath the portico. It was afternoon now and the golden columns threw dark shadowed bars across the walkway. As Flavia climbed down from the litter, she noticed for the first time that the bearers were female.

Holding her beribboned tambourine, Flavia followed one of the female bearers into a huge domed space.

"The octagonal room," breathed Flavia, tipping her head back and putting up her free hand to keep the garland on her head. The immense dome and large circular skylight gave the room a breathtaking sense of space and light. Beneath the dome, dozens of dark-haired women worked at colorful tapestries. Some of them had already put down their shuttles, beaters, and wool; they were beginning to form a semicircle around a central platform beneath the dome.

"That's where you sit," the litter bearer said to Flavia, indicating the platform. "Play half a dozen songs," she continued in a husky voice, "take a break, play six more, then we'll carry you back to the Palatine. Oh, and if the Emperor appears, you don't need to bow or acknowledge him in any way. Unless, of course, he approaches you. In which case, the correct way to address him is 'Caesar.'"

"All right," murmured Flavia politely. She led the other two up to the platform, where cushions were already set out.

"This is it," she whispered to Nubia and Lupus. "Keep your eyes open for Jonathan or Simeon. Or anything suspicious."

■■■

As Susannah the Beautiful approached, Jonathan took a deep breath and stepped out from behind the bush.

"Oh!" she cried out and her hand went to her throat. Then she saw Rizpah and spoke in Aramaic.

"Rizpah! You frightened me. You mustn't leap out of the shrubbery like that."

"I'm sorry, Susannah." Rizpah shaded her eyes with both hands and screwed up her face against the brilliance of the garden.

"Who's this?" asked Susannah, looking at Jonathan with interest, but before either of them could answer, her eyes widened.

"Jonathan?" she whispered. "Is it you?"

Nubia glanced at Lupus and Flavia to make sure they were ready. They nodded back at her and she lifted the flute to her lips.

First they played the "Song of the Traveler," a song from Nubia's native land. Then they played "The Raven and the Dove," a song their friend Clio had taught them. Under Nubia's fingers this popular song took on an exotic flavor.

Nubia set aside her flute to sing the "Dog Song," while Lupus drummed; then she and Flavia took up their instruments again for the last two songs, both of which Nubia had composed herself. The first she called "Sailing Song" and the second, her favorite, she called "Slave Song." She could never play this last without shedding a tear and when she looked up she saw that most of the women from Jerusalem also had wet cheeks.

Nubia felt a touch on her arm. Flavia nodded toward a man standing behind them on the extreme left, leaning against one of the golden columns.

The man's eyes were closed and his face turned up toward the diffused light of the dome.

Although he wasn't wearing his purple toga or golden wreath this time, Nubia recognized him. "Titus?" she whispered.

Flavia nodded.

■■■

Jonathan tried not to cry out as his mother threw her arms around him, but he couldn't help flinching.

"Oh, Jonathan!" she drew back and looked at his shoulder in horror. "I've hurt you. Dear Lord! Titus didn't say you'd been branded! Oh my poor son."

"The Emperor knows about me?" said Jonathan, taking a step back. Although she had spoken to him in Aramaic he used Latin.

"Of course." She followed his lead and replied in Latin. "They look for you everywhere." Her Latin wasn't very good. "Simeon tells us how brave you've been, how you are willing to risk your life—"

"Simeon? He's all right? They haven't tortured and blinded him?"

"No, no." Susannah stepped forward and took Jonathan's face between her cool hands. He caught a whiff of her scent. It was no longer lemon blossom, but something different: rose and myrtle. "Your uncle Simeon is good," she said. "He is on the Palatine. Josephus warns Titus before they torture him."

"Josephus!" Jonathan stepped back again, away from her touch. "That's the name of the man who betrayed us."

His mother let her arms fall to her sides. "Josephus doesn't know Simeon comes to help," she said. "He thinks your uncle assassinates the Emperor. Josephus is loyal to Emperor."

"And I see that you are loyal to the Emperor, too."

"Jonathan. Do not hate Titus. He is good man."

"He murdered thousands of Jews, destroyed Jerusalem, and burned down God's temple!" cried Jonathan.

"And he is most sorry."

"Oh. He's sorry. Well then. That makes it all right, doesn't it? So now you can kiss him and tell him it doesn't matter."

"Jonathan. Please do not."

He turned his head aside, fighting to hold back the tears. "I came to find you. To warn you. To take you back to Miriam and Father. And I find you in the arms of that monster . . ."

"Jonathan. You are dear, precious son. I am so sorry." She took his hands. "Please, my Jonathan. Tell me. How is sister Miriam? And Father? And you?"

Lupus was watching one of the slave women closely. He had noticed her even before they began to play. The way she had walked to her cushion had attracted his attention. Was she Jonathan's mother? No. There was no look of Miriam or Jonathan about her face.

Perhaps he had seen her somewhere before?

As he drummed he let his gaze slide around the other women's faces. Most had their eyes closed or were weeping. But this woman's eyes beneath her black headscarf were cool and calculating; unaffected, even by the "Slave Song."

She must have felt his gaze, for as she looked at him she modestly covered the lower half of her face with her scarf. For a moment their gazes locked. That's odd, thought Lupus: One of her eyes is half brown and half blue.

SCROLL XXIII

"Alas! My heart is wretched." Lupus heard Nubia whisper to Flavia. "Because I have no more songs. They will know we are not real music players."

"Don't worry, Nubia. We'll just play them again."

Lupus saw that the Emperor was approaching their low platform. At the same time he noticed the woman with the strange eye had risen to her feet. Another woman—one with fluffy brown hair—gripped her hand, but the first woman shook it off and walked slowly toward the golden portico.

The Emperor was standing before them now, talking to Flavia. Lupus ignored him, turned his head to watch the woman move toward the columns. He knew there was something else strange about her.

Just before she disappeared from sight, a breeze blew up the hem of her black robes. Lupus saw a hairy and well-muscled calf, and below it, a soldier's sandal.

Rizpah must have slipped back into the shadows because Jonathan sensed that he and his mother were alone now. He sat on the chair the Emperor had occupied earlier and allowed her to hold his hands.

Jonathan reverted to Hebrew to tell his mother about his

childhood without her, how they had moved from Pella to Rome and then to Ostia. He told her about Flavia, Lupus, and Nubia. He told her that Miriam was engaged to a Roman farmer who had probably lost everything in the eruption of Vesuvius. He told her his father was well, but lonely.

Finally, Jonathan told his mother how he had dreamed of her in the cave of the Cyclops, waiting to be rescued.

"Mother. It was my fault that you stayed in Jerusalem and were taken captive. But now I can fix it. I think I can find a way for us to get out of here."

"You do?" she said vaguely, and then: "But, Jonathan, why do you think it was your fault?"

"Simeon said you stayed in Jerusalem because of me."

"What?"

"I overheard Simeon tell Father you stayed in Jerusalem because of me."

His mother turned her head and stared into the cave of the Cyclops.

"Then he knows."

"What are you talking about? What did I do to make you stay?"

"No." She looked back at him and he saw that her eyes were full of tears. "It wasn't you, my son. Nothing was your fault. You were only a toddler. A dear, sweet little boy."

"Then . . . I don't understand."

His mother stood. She walked to her loom and reached out to touch the wool stretched taut across it.

"I did a bad thing, Jonathan. I never wanted you or Miriam or your father to know."

"What? What did you do, Mother?"

Jonathan's mother looked at him and then beyond him. He turned to see what she was looking at.

A figure stood in the bright garden, watching them through the columns. It was one of the Jewish slave women. She was dressed in black and had pulled her scarf across her face. It seemed one of the women of Jerusalem had come to offer her hand in friendship.

Then his mother's dark blue eyes opened in surprise. Following her gaze, Jonathan saw that the woman in black came not in friendship but in malice.

In her hand she held a curved, razor-sharp dagger.

"Aiieeee!" Lupus struck the assassin at the back of the knees.

"Oof!" The figure in black collapsed.

Lupus rolled aside to avoid being crushed, grasped the figure's headscarf, and yanked. Long hair tumbled out as the assassin's head flew up and then cracked down hard onto the marble walkway.

Lupus's flowered garland had slipped down over his eyes. With a grunt of disgust he tore it from his head and threw it away. Luckily, the figure on the floor was stunned. Lupus saw long hair and heavy eye-liner, but the stubble on the assassin's cheeks confirmed what Lupus had suspected: It was a man. And although he was fine-boned with delicate features, he was tough. Already he was shaking his head and struggling to sit up.

The knife.

Lupus had to get the knife away from the assassin. He had just lunged for it when a foot stomped hard on the assassin's wrist. The knife spun across the shaded marble path and into the shadows of a cavelike room.

"Lupus! Give me your hand!" The voice was Jonathan's.

Lupus grasped an extended hand and was pulled to his feet.

It took him a split second to recognize the slave boy who had helped him up. Jonathan seemed taller and thinner. His shaved head made his eyes look huge. And he had a strange expression on his face.

Lupus grunted and leaped back as the assassin struggled to his feet. Then for a second time he kicked the man hard in the back of the knees. The man went down again, this time onto all fours, his long hair screening his face.

"Jonathan!" Lupus heard a little girl's voice and the sound of metal on marble and suddenly Jonathan held the dagger in his hand. Someone in the shadows had kicked it back to him.

Still on all fours, the man in the black robes looked up. Jonathan was breathing hard, half crouching and holding the curved dagger in his right hand. Somewhere a woman was screaming. Lupus could hear the approaching slap of running feet on marble and the sound of a jingling tambourine.

So could the assassin.

He looked around like a cornered beast, his long hair flying about his shoulders. Then he rose and turned and ran through the garden courtyard toward the vaulted rooms near the front of the palace.

Lupus ran after him.

Jonathan knew he had to get his mother to safety. As soon as he saw the assassin fleeing, he ran up to her. She was cowering in the shadows behind her loom.

"Come on, Mother! I know where we can hide," he said, then turned in amazement as he heard a familiar voice shout:

"There he is!"

As if in a dream he saw Flavia and Nubia run through the sunlit garden. They were both wearing flowered garlands with colored ribbons streaming out behind. Flavia held a beribboned tambourine in one hand; it jingled as she ran. Neither of them saw him standing in the shadowed vault, gripping his mother's wrist.

Two muscular women in shiny breastplates came hard on the girls' heels and then the Emperor himself, red-faced and gasping.

"Titus!" whispered Jonathan's mother. She took a step forward, but Jonathan pulled her back, almost roughly. Still holding her by the wrist, he set off through several dim, empty rooms, pulling her after him.

"Where are we going?"

"Here." He pulled her into a small triangular room. He remembered Rizpah telling him Nero had once used it to display a statue of a sleeping satyr, but now the room was empty.

Jonathan stopped, panting hard. "We'll be safe here for a while. Then Rizpah will show us the way out." Still holding her hand, Jonathan turned to his mother. "First, tell me . . . what was the bad thing you did?" His breath came in wheezing gasps. "Why didn't you . . . escape with us?"

His mother looked at him and then dropped her head.

"There was a man," she finally said.

"A man?"

"I loved him."

Jonathan realized he was still holding her hand. He dropped it.

"He was a famous freedom fighter. His name was on everyone's lips. They called him Jonathan the Zealot."

"His name was Jonathan?"

She nodded.

The odd shape of the room made him feel slightly unbalanced, and not for the first time, he wondered if he was dreaming.

"Am I . . . named after him?"

His mother hung her head and nodded again.

Jonathan felt cold. He could see each black and white chip in the mosaic floor with terrible clarity. Finally he took a deep breath and asked: "Was Jonathan the Zealot my real father?"

SCROLL XXIV

"There he is!" shouted Flavia.

When Lupus had jumped off the platform she had followed him without hesitation. She hadn't even put down her tambourine.

She and Nubia had run down the colonnade after Lupus, the golden columns flashing by on their left. Suddenly Lupus had veered right, and they followed him across a hot, grassy courtyard, into a complex of brightly painted, high-vaulted rooms. There they lost him, until a woman's scream directed them to an inner garden courtyard. A moment later a long-haired man in black robes ran past, closely pursued by Lupus.

Flavia heard footsteps behind her and glanced back. Two of the muscular female litter bearers and Titus himself had joined the chase.

"There he is!" she shouted to them again.

She followed Lupus through a large vaulted room and suddenly they were at the front of the palace again, at the golden portico.

Flavia stopped for a moment, hugged one of the golden columns with her left arm, and looked around, panting. There! The assassin was splashing through the reflecting pool, sending the exotic pink birds into a panic. They squawked and flapped and tried to fly away, but in vain: Their wings had been clipped.

Suddenly the man slipped and fell with a splash, then staggered to his feet. His black robes clung to his body and they could see his masculine build. Lupus was almost upon him now. Flavia gasped as the assassin swung around to strike Lupus a glancing backhand blow.

"Lupus!" She pushed away from the column and ran to help him, Nubia close beside her.

Lupus had fallen into the pool. But a moment later he was up, shaking himself off like a dog, then resuming his pursuit of the assassin, who had doubled back and was running up marble stairs to the upper level. Flavia and Nubia were close behind Lupus now, close enough to see drops of water flying off his soaked green tunic.

Flavia took the stairs two at a time, her tambourine jingling with each step, trying not to slip on the scattered pine needles.

"Behold!" Nubia panted, and Flavia caught a glimpse of the assassin turning to run along the long upper portico of white columns. Lupus was right behind him.

Hampered by his dripping black robes, the assassin was running awkwardly now; once he almost tripped. He stumbled along the portico, then veered between the columns and into a small, angular garden. Beyond a circle of palm trees in the center of the garden, Flavia saw another portico with thick green woods beyond. Woods thick enough to hide any fugitive.

The assassin saw it, too, and made for it, heading toward the ring of palms.

Suddenly Flavia remembered the plans she had studied with Sisyphus. There was a click in her mind, like the sound of a wax seal being broken. She knew what the palm trees surrounded and which room was below them.

"Lupus!" she cried. "The eye! It's inside the palm trees. Be careful!"

Lupus heard her, but so did the assassin. The man skidded to a halt, then whirled to face them, his long hair flying. He crouched and his eyes narrowed as he saw his closest pursuer was just a boy.

Flavia knew she had to act quickly, before the assassin could attack Lupus. She drew back her arm and threw her tambourine hard, like a discus, giving it a spin as it left her hand. Amazingly, it went exactly where she had intended: The beribboned tambourine struck the assassin a hard jingling blow on the chest, then bounced to the ground. The man staggered back, flailing wildly with his arms, trying to keep his balance.

Then he was gone.

Flavia and Nubia ran to the rim of the eye, the circular skylight in the dome. A shower of dust and gravel rattled over the side and disappeared into the octagonal room below. Lupus was breathing hard, hands on his knees, gazing down into the void below. The female guards and finally the Emperor himself came puffing up behind them.

"Careful!" cried Flavia. But they knew the layout of the Golden House and slowed down before they reached the rim of the circular gap.

If there had ever been glass in the skylight, it must have been stripped away, along with other precious materials. The man in black had plunged sixty feet and had hit the platform where they had been playing music a few minutes earlier. His long hair fanned out across his back, giving him the look of a jointed wooden doll that a child has thrown down in disgust. It was obvious from the impossible angle of his head that his neck was broken.

The assassin was dead.

In a triangular room somewhere near the back of the Golden House Jonathan asked his mother: "Was Jonathan the Zealot my real father?"

"No." His mother raised her head. "You are Mordecai's son. I hadn't been unfaithful to him." She lowered her eyes again. "Not then."

"Then how? When?"

His mother turned to face the plaster wall. There was a fresco of Venus on it and she reached up to touch the goddess's face.

"Jonathan was the first man I had ever met who wasn't a close relative," she said. "I was fourteen and he was seventeen, a few months older than Simeon. The two of them had been throwing rocks at the Romans and some soldiers were chasing them. They ran into our house and I hid them behind my loom. Jonathan had hurt his hand so while Simeon went out of the room to see if it was safe, I dressed Jonathan's wound. While Simeon was gone, in only a few short moments, Jonathan kissed me and told me I was the most beautiful woman he'd ever seen. He said he wanted to marry me. He was young, brave, handsome . . . Even then his name was whispered by all the girls. I was dazzled."

Jonathan felt unsteady and had to lean against the wall. His mother still had her back to him.

"A few days later," she continued, "my father said a man had asked to marry me. I was overjoyed. Then father told me he was a doctor, a man of twenty-seven, and my heart sank. I heard nothing more from Jonathan, so I married the doctor, your father. He was a kind man. We went to live in his house near the Beautiful Gate. Soon I had the two of you. I was not unhappy."

"You were not unhappy," repeated Jonathan dully.

"Miriam was born the year the rebellion started. It was the same year your father joined that sect. While everyone praised the bravery of Jonathan the Zealot, all your father talked about was loving our enemies."

"Go on," said Jonathan.

"One day, I was visiting my parents when Simeon and Jonathan came in from one of their secret missions against the Romans. It was the first time I had seen Jonathan in nearly five years. I watched him from behind a latticework screen. 'Have you heard?' Jonathan was saying to my father. 'The Christians are leaving the city. Going across the Jordan, to Pella. I hope your son-in-law isn't one of them. Cowards!' My father didn't say anything but I could tell by the way he clenched his jaw that he agreed with Jonathan. 'I should have accepted your offer to marry Susannah,' he said to Jonathan. 'I didn't want a Zealot as a son-in-law. But it would have been preferable to one of those madmen who think God had a son.' That was when I realized Jonathan had asked to marry me."

Susannah was silent for a moment. Then she continued. "As soon as my father left the room, I stepped out from behind the screen. Jonathan ran to me and told me he had never stopped loving me and that he would die for me. We said many other things. When I finally returned home that day I found your father about to flee the city. He begged me to come but I refused, saying that my father had forbidden me to leave. I let him go. And I let him take you with him."

"So you loved Jonathan more than you loved us," said Jonathan in a flat voice. He felt sick.

"I don't think it was love." His mother leaned her cheek against the wall. "It was a kind of madness. The next week the gates of Jerusalem were closed and the armies of Titus encamped outside. Jonathan and I had a few weeks together, maybe a month. We lived secretly in your father's house, for I was still a married woman and adultery was a crime punishable by death. Then the famine set in. One day Jonathan went out and never returned. I heard later that he was killed fighting a man for a piece of dead mule. A brave death," she said bitterly.

She turned to face Jonathan. Her eyes were dry.

"That's the reason I didn't come with you."

"But now . . ." said Jonathan, "now I've come to rescue you. To take you home."

"Jonathan. My dear brave Jonathan. I can't come with you. I must stay here."

"Why?"

"Titus needs me."

"We need you! I need you. I came all this way to bring you home."

"I can't."

For a moment it was as if Jonathan was standing above the scene. He could see himself: thin, pale, his head shaved and an angry red brand on his arm. He looked like a slave. And his mother standing with her head bent before him. He saw that he was almost as tall as she was.

"Can you forgive me, Jonathan?"

He stared at her. He had risked his life to save her and now she refused to escape with him. Just as she had refused his father ten years earlier.

"Please, Jonathan?"

Slowly Jonathan shook his head. Then he turned and stumbled out of the room. He ran along the cryptoporticus, and although he was half blinded by tears, somehow he found the dark tunnels Rizpah had shown him. Like a mole, he made his way blindly along them until he found the darkest, most hidden place of all.

SCROLL XXV

"Flavia Gemina," said the Emperor, mopping his brow.

Flavia glanced over at the Emperor in amazement. They were all walking back along the golden portico toward the octagonal room. The Emperor's sandy curls were plastered to his pink forehead and he was breathing as hard as a bull led to sacrifice.

"How do you know my name, Caesar?" she stammered.

"I have an . . . excellent memory." Now he was mopping his chin and neck. "I met you . . . at the refugee camp . . . south of Stabia . . . Your uncle—Flavius Geminus—was with you."

"That's right," said Flavia.

"And you're her slave girl . . . Sheba."

"Nubia."

"That's right. Nubia." He looked at Lupus. "And Lupus. A most . . . unusual name."

"That's amazing," said Flavia. "That you should remember our names."

"Confession," the Emperor said. "Jonathan's uncle Simeon . . . mentioned you . . . Told me you were the boy's friends."

"Simeon!" cried Flavia. They had reached the octagonal room and she stopped beside one of the golden columns. "He's an assassin, Caesar. He's going to kill you," she gestured with her tambourine, "like that man just tried to kill you."

"No." The Emperor smiled. "But I appreciate your loyalty in telling me. Simeon came to warn me, not to kill me. You see, it was his own sister—Jonathan's mother—he was sent to assassinate. That assassin intended to kill Susannah. Not me."

"Yes, he did intend to kill you," said a voice. It was a woman's voice, full of hatred.

The women of Jerusalem stood around the platform in the middle of the octagonal room, looking down at the dead assassin. One of them was kneeling beside his broken body and it was she who had spoken. She had dark, fluffy hair and narrow eyes full of hatred.

Titus walked to the platform and frowned down at her.

"My name is Rachel," she said, rising to her feet. "But you wouldn't know that, even though I've been your slave for nine years. His name was Pinchas. I only knew him a few hours but in that short time I could tell he was a brave man. One of our freedom fighters. Berenice hired him to kill that traitor Susannah. But afterwards he was going to kill you, too. He was a true hero. You are a pig."

Slowly and deliberately, Rachel spat in the Emperor's face.

Everyone gasped and stared at him.

Then Titus did something Flavia would never forget.

"You may not believe this, Rachel," he said quietly, mopping his cheek with his handkerchief, "but I would rather be killed than kill one more person. I am sorry this man is dead. And I am truly sorry for what I had to do to your country. To your people."

He looked around at them all. "You are not my slaves but Berenice's. But she will not return." He hung his head for a moment and Flavia was close enough to hear him murmur, "I should have done this before."

The Emperor raised his head again and continued in his commander's voice. "I hereby set you all free. You may remain here as my freedwomen, under my protection, and begin to receive wages for your weaving. Or you may go. The decision is yours."

He started to turn away, and then added, "If you stay, I will allow you to marry. I believe Berenice was only trying to protect you by keeping you from men. Because whether you believe it or not, she loved you all. Her parting wish was that I watch over you."

He turned away from the women of Jerusalem and said to Flavia and her friends, "Come, Flavia Gemina. Let us find your friend Jonathan."

But though they searched and searched, Jonathan was nowhere to be found.

Jonathan remained in his dark hole for a long time. There was barely enough room for him to sit, so he curled up and huddled there. Thoughts raced around and around his head, like chariots at the circus. Presently he slept and dreamed of his childhood. He woke and sought refuge in sleep again; the dreams were the most vivid he had ever had.

Someone regularly left a jug of fresh water outside the entrance, but nobody spoke to him and it seemed that he was alone for weeks.

What finally drove him out was the hunger.

He was sick and dizzy with it, and as he wormed his way along the tunnel he had to stop every few minutes and gasp for breath. Once or twice his throat contracted and he almost retched. He could taste the bitter juices of his empty stomach.

At last he staggered blinking into the cryptoporticus and stared toward the light in wonder.

A figure stood there. The filtered sunlight behind her made her white hair and her white tunic glow like an aura around her.

"Rizpah?" he croaked.

She nodded, and stepped forward. She handed him a jug of cold water. In the crook of her arm she cradled a gray kitten.

"How long have I been in there?" he asked her after he had drained the jug.

"Three days."

"Only three days?" Jonathan slumped down onto the floor and leaned the back of his head against the cool plaster of the cryptoporticus. "It feels like weeks."

"No," said Rizpah, sitting beside him. "Only three days."

"I'm ravenous," he turned his head to look at her. "Have you got any bread?"

"No," she was stroking the kitten. "No food today. We're all fasting."

"What?"

"Today is Yom Kippur," she said. "The Day of Atonement. Everyone here in the Golden House is fasting. But don't worry. We'll eat this evening."

He gulped some air and tried to stand. But he felt too dizzy and let his back slide slowly down the wall again.

"How is my mother?" he asked after a while.

"Waiting for you. They all are. The Emperor and your friends looked everywhere and finally they went away. I didn't tell them where you were but I told them you were all right."

"Will you take me to her?"

"Of course." She wrinkled her nose. "But first you might want to visit the baths."

"All right," said Jonathan. "You lead the way and I'll crawl after you."

SCROLL XXVI

"Please, Mother. Tell me why you won't come back to Ostia with me." Jonathan sat facing his mother in the shaded peristyle by the cave of the Cyclops. He had bathed in hot sulphur water and cold seawater. Now, dressed in a loose white tunic, he felt clean and new, though the brand on his left arm throbbed and his stomach was empty as a pit.

His barefoot mother was also dressed in white: a long linen tunic, unbelted because leather could not be worn on the Day of Atonement.

"Tell me why you can't come home with me," he repeated.

She nodded. "I'll try to explain," she said and took his cold hands in her warm ones. "After the famine set in, the nightmare began. My lover Jonathan died, as I told you, fighting over a dead mule. After that, I went to stay with my parents. About this time Simeon became a Christian, like your father. He renounced the Zealots and came to stay with us. Simeon and I watched our parents slowly weaken and die. There was nothing we could do to help them. We cooked belts, sandals, even scrolls. My mother died first, then my father. As my father lay dying I held him in my arms. He looked up at me and said, 'I know you committed a sin which demands the penalty of death. God forgive me, Susannah, I could not stone my own daughter.' I wept when I realized he knew what I had done.

'Atone for your sins,' he whispered. 'Obey the Lord and follow his commandments.' I nodded. 'I promise I'll be good from now on.' He died smiling."

Susannah squeezed Jonathan's hands and he looked up at her.

"Jonathan," she said. "I know God spared me for a reason. I honored my father's dying wish. I have spent most of the past nine years at my loom in silent prayer. Somehow I knew you had all survived. I prayed for you every day. I prayed for everyone I knew, even Titus."

Jonathan nodded. He could smell her rose and myrtle perfume.

"Then, last year, Titus sent Berenice away. But I know he missed her because he used to come back here and wander through the rooms she had occupied. One day he walked through the octagonal room. Most of the women turned their faces away, but I smiled at him as I prayed for him. The next day he summoned me into his presence."

Jonathan swallowed. His heart was pounding.

"I think at first that he wanted me to take Berenice's place. But we ended up talking. It became a regular occurrence. He especially likes hearing about our Torah. He is intrigued that our God is a moral one. Titus has committed many great sins, as I have. He does not fully believe, but he is beginning to."

Jonathan looked at her. "Then he's not your lover?"

She looked at him and for the first time he saw complete openness in her eyes. "No. We are not lovers. Only friends."

Jonathan breathed a sigh of relief. That meant she had changed. That meant there was hope. Hope that she might yet come back to them.

"Jonathan," she was saying. "I am atoning for my sins. For letting my father down, my husband, my children. I would dearly love to come home to you but I believe God has led me here, to the most powerful man in the world, for such a time as this. Do you understand?"

Jonathan shook his head. "Not really."

She squeezed his hands again, and looked down at them. "My ring!" she exclaimed. "Jonathan, where did you find my ring?"

Jonathan looked in surprise at the sardonyx ring on his little finger.

"Oh," he said. "I was looking through your things, trying to find out what happened to you. I found this," he slipped it easily off his finger. "And I found love letters that father wrote to you. Beautiful love letters quoting the Song of Solomon." Suddenly a terrible thought occurred to him. "Or did Jonathan write them?"

"No." Tears filled her eyes. "Your father wrote those letters to me."

Jonathan nodded and hung his head so she would not see his face.

Presently he slid the ring onto the forefinger of her left hand. "Here," he said. "Take it. Promise me you'll wear it. And whenever you catch sight of it, will you think of me?"

"I have thought of you every day," she whispered. "Every day since the last time I saw you, looking over your father's shoulder, waving good-bye to me with your chubby hand."

The octagonal court had been cleared of looms. There were too many diners for couches, so long tables had been brought in and every chair and stool available. It was just past dusk and a hundred candles and oil lamps filled the deep blue of the domed room with stars of light.

Two hundred slave women and twenty-four children, all in white, sat at long tables, ready to eat the food set before them. Jonathan sat between Rizpah and the slave boy called Benjamin. On Rizpah's right was her mother, Rachel—the woman with fluffy brown hair who had spat in Titus's face. She sat quietly and gazed thoughtfully at the candles.

Jonathan's stomach rumbled fiercely as he caught a whiff of

roast chicken and coriander. He was dizzy with hunger.

There was a murmur at the table as two figures in white entered the room through the golden columns: a man and a woman.

Jonathan knew the woman was his mother, but the man didn't look like Titus.

"Is it Titus?" Jonathan peered into the gloom. "I can't see clearly in this light."

"No," whispered Rizpah. "It is a tall, slim man."

"Uncle Simeon!" cried Jonathan.

His uncle stepped into the lamplight at the head of the table, and gave Jonathan his radiant gap-toothed smile.

"Before Susannah recites the blessing," Simeon said in his deep voice, "I have some news to give you. Titus has just made me steward of this house. As you know, the Emperor set you free three days ago. You are now his freedwomen, under his protection for as long as you choose. You will be given quarters here and elsewhere, and you will be allowed to marry."

He looked around at them all. "You are probably wondering who I am. My name is Simeon ben Jonah. Susannah here is my sister. For half a year you have shunned her for befriending the Emperor. But today is the day when God wipes our sins from his memory and writes our names in his scroll of life."

"Will you forgive her, at last, and receive her back into your company?"

There was a positive murmur and then Rizpah's mother stood and looked around at them all. "None of us is without sin," she said. "We forgive you, Susannah." Rachel smiled at Susannah and Simeon, then resumed her seat.

Jonathan's mother remained standing. She lifted her veil and covered her head, and she looked so much like Miriam that Jonathan wanted to cry.

"Let us eat and be glad," she said with a smile.

As Jonathan began to eat, he felt his spirits lift.

"It takes so little," he said.

"What?" said Rizpah. Her pale eyes looked pink in the lamplight.

"A few bites of food make us happy again. Food is a wonderful thing."

"Yes," said Rizpah. "Food is wonderful."

Jonathan took a mouthful of chicken. "I suppose you'll be leaving here with your mother. After what she said to the Emperor today. You'll miss your tunnels, won't you."

"Oh, I don't think we'll be leaving here," said Rizpah with a smile, and glanced at her mother. "Not if your handsome uncle is remaining as steward. No," said Rizpah, popping a bean into her mouth. "Here I was born and here I'll die."

SCROLL XXVII

"Caesar," said Jonathan, and rose from the couch.

"No, don't get up, Jonathan. Sit. I need to talk to you."

It was late morning of the Sabbath. Jonathan had spent the night in a luxurious guest room on the Palatine Hill.

Jonathan sat back down on the edge of the couch and the Emperor sat beside him. For a moment Jonathan and the Emperor Titus both looked at the painting on the wall opposite. The fresco showed the return of Odysseus in the moment where he discards the disguise of a beggar to reveal his true identity.

"I have fought in many battles," said Titus presently, "and many have called me brave. But what you did in coming here to find your mother, risking torture and possibly death—that was remarkable."

Jonathan looked down. "Thank you," he said.

"Jonathan. Your mother is teaching me so much." The Emperor looked down at his hands, at the thick fingers covered with rings. "She is a very wise and beautiful woman."

Jonathan kept his eyes down.

The Emperor reached out his right hand and almost touched the brand on Jonathan's left shoulder.

"I'm sorry about this, Jonathan."

Jonathan looked away and shrugged. "I belong to you. I'm Caesar's slave now."

"No." The Emperor fished in a pouch at his belt and pulled

out Jonathan's ruby ring and bulla. "You are not my slave." He held them out to Jonathan. "I release you from servitude to me and I grant you not only your freedom, Jonathan, but your citizenship."

Slowly, Jonathan took his ring and bulla. Roman citizenship was a precious and sought-after gift.

"You're too young to receive it now, but I will bestow that honor upon your father. Then your whole family will be citizens. By the way, your father is no longer in prison."

"My father was in prison?"

"The magistrate in Ostia took him in for questioning. Your friends told me and I sent word that he be released at once. As a Roman citizen he will of course have special privileges. This sort of thing should never happen to him again."

"Thank you."

The Emperor removed one of the rings from his little finger. "Take this ring, too. If anyone questions the brand on your shoulder, mistakes you for my slave, show them this. It proves that you are no longer a slave but under my protection. And if you should ever need anything, you have only to come to the Palatine and present that ring. I will see you at once."

Jonathan nodded and glanced at the Emperor. He could see his eyelashes and the mixture of green, gold, and brown in his hazel eyes. For the first time he saw Titus as a man and not as the Emperor.

"Thank you," said Jonathan. And he took the ring.

Beneath the grape arbor in the house of Senator Cornix, Sisyphus the Greek secretary took the message from Bulbus and thumbed the parchment open. The seal fell off and rattled onto the table like a small wax coin.

Flavia picked up the disc of red wax and studied it as Sisyphus scanned the message. Titus's seal was the boar of the tenth legion, the legion he had commanded in Judaea. Underneath it were the letters IMP TITVS CAES VESP.

"It's in Titus's own hand," said Sisyphus, raising his eyebrows. "He thanks us for our loyalty and devotion to him and to the Roman Empire. He says that our friend Jonathan is rested and well," Sisyphus looked up in surprise, "and already on his way back to Ostia."

SCROLL XXVIII

Jonathan lay on a rush mat between Flavia and Nubia and looked up at the chinks of turquoise sky gleaming through the lattice of branches. Tigris was curled up at his feet panting gently with his pink tongue. It was the next to last day of September, and the three friends were back in Ostia, lying beneath a shelter woven of branches in Jonathan's garden.

"So," said Flavia quietly. "Your mother is alive."

"Yes. You and Nubia and Lupus saved her life."

"So did you. If you hadn't gone to Rome . . ."

Jonathan grunted.

"And your father doesn't know?" whispered Flavia.

"No," said Jonathan. "He doesn't know she's alive. She asked me not to tell him. Yet."

"I hope we can go back to Rome again one day," said Flavia. "I'd like to meet her."

"I have a feeling," said Jonathan, "that we'll go back."

Flavia reached up and brushed a green palm frond with the tips of her fingers. "So what's this thing called again?"

"A sukkah. The word means shelter. It's supposed to remind us of the time the Jewish people wandered in the desert. Before we found the promised land."

"So this is another festival."

"Yes. We call it the Feast of Tabernacles. A tabernacle is a tent or a shelter like this."

"What are those dates hanging from roof?" asked Nubia.

Jonathan grinned. "They're for you."

Nubia sat up and reached for one.

"And we're going to eat dinner in here tonight?" said Flavia.

"Yes." Jonathan sat up. "Miriam's cooking my favorite stew again. I didn't eat much of it on my birthday."

Flavia sat up too, hugged her knees, and inhaled. "I like it in here. It smells lovely."

"And you can see the sky," added Nubia.

"Yes," said Jonathan. "You're supposed to be able to see the stars at night." He reached up and pulled a few grapes from a cluster hanging above his head.

"You sleeping here?" asked Nubia, her amber eyes gleaming with interest.

Jonathan nodded. "It's the full moon tonight."

"Can we sleep here, too?" cried Flavia.

"I'll have to ask Father but I think he'll say yes. It's big enough for us all."

"Do you all sleep out here?"

"Of course. For eight nights we eat and sleep in the sukkah. Me and Miriam and Father and Lupus."

Nubia frowned. "Where is the Lupus?"

"He had a visitor just before you arrived. A man in a green tunic with his hair all oiled and combed back. He looked like one of Felix's men. They went off toward the harbor."

"Hey!" cried Flavia. "Two weeks ago Lupus told us that Felix was looking for something for him. Maybe he's found it."

"He did indeed," said a voice from outside the shelter.

"What is it, Father?" Jonathan emerged from the succah, followed by Flavia and Nubia. Mordecai was thin and pale, but smiling. He held a tray with cups of mint tea on it and gestured with his bearded chin toward the front of the house.

They all saw Lupus step into the bright inner garden, hand in hand with a small dark-haired girl.

"Great Neptune's beard," breathed Jonathan. "It's Clio."

"Clio!" Flavia squealed with delight and ran to hug the little girl. "You weren't buried by the volcano!"

Clio grinned and shook her head.

"It's thanks to her we survived," said a woman's voice. "She insisted we all clamber over the landslide and walk to Neapolis."

"Rectina!" said Flavia. "You're alive, too! And all eight of Clio's sisters?"

Rectina nodded and smiled. She was a tall, elegant woman with beautiful dark eyes.

"Where are they?" said Flavia, looking behind Rectina, and then stopped as she saw a man and a girl standing in the shadowed corridor. Flavia's heart skipped a beat and she barely heard Rectina's answer: "My husband and Vulcan and the girls are all in Stabia, helping with the relief operations."

Flavia nodded vaguely at Rectina and moved past her. "Hello, Pulchra," she said. "Hello, Patron."

"Flavia darling," cried the blonde girl. She stepped forward and managed to kiss Flavia on both cheeks without touching either of them. For a moment they looked into each other's eyes. Then they both grinned and hugged each other tightly.

"Jonathan!" Pulchra thrust Flavia aside and rushed forward into the sunshine.

Flavia staggered and laughed and watched Pulchra hug Jonathan. Then she turned back to the man standing in the shadows. He was tall and tanned, with dark eyes and prematurely gray hair.

"Hello, Flavia Gemina," he said. "Are you well?"

"Very well," said Flavia, touching her hair to make sure it was tidy.

Publius Pollius Felix was wearing a sky-blue tunic and a short gray traveling cloak. He looked even more handsome than she remembered. Flavia swallowed. "Were you the one who found Clio? Was that what you were looking for? For Lupus, I mean?"

Felix nodded and smiled at the group of friends in the sunlit garden, all chattering and hugging and writing on wax tablets. "I had my men looking everywhere. Then one day I had to visit my estate at Pausilypon and I rode into Neapolis to do some business. A colleague there told me the story of a woman and her nine daughters who had escaped the volcano on foot. I knew it had to be them."

"They walked all the way to Neapolis?" Flavia pulled a myrtle twig from her hair and let it drop on the ground behind her.

Felix nodded. "It's only about four miles. But they made the right decision. By the worst stage of the eruption, they were safely out of danger. Now they are reunited, and helping me with the relief operations. Tascius and Rectina have adopted two more orphans."

"Girls?" asked Flavia.

Felix smiled. "One of each, actually."

"Hey," said Flavia, looking back over her shoulder at the happy crowd. "Where's Miriam?"

"I brought your uncle Gaius back with me," said Felix, half turning toward the atrium. "I believe Miriam is greeting him."

"Oh," said Flavia. And then, "Oh!"

Felix gave her an amused glance.

"Hello, Patron." Jonathan stepped forward and held out his hand.

"Hello, Jonathan." Felix grasped his hand. "Are you well? You look . . . older."

"I am older," said Jonathan. "I celebrated my eleventh birthday a few weeks ago."

"Congratulations."

"Patron, I would like to invite you and Pulchra to dine with us this evening under the sukkah."

Felix looked over Jonathan's shoulder at the shelter woven of palm, myrtle, and willow. Beside it, Nubia was introducing Clio to Pulchra.

"It looks as if it might be an interesting experience," said Felix. "Pulchra and I would be honored to stay for dinner."

Jonathan looked around his sukkah with satisfaction. He had built it well. In a few days it would begin to grow stiff and yellow and the fruit would wither, but for now it was good. The branches were green and supple and fragrant. The fruit hanging from the woven canopy was ripe and full of sweet juices. And there was room for everyone. They sat on embroidered cushions around the octagonal table and sipped their watered wine and chatted as they waited for the dessert course.

His sister Miriam looked beautiful in her white tunic. Whenever he looked at her now, he saw his mother. Miriam and Gaius were speaking softly, as lovers do, oblivious of everyone else.

Clio was dressed in a bright orange tunic, chattering away to Lupus, describing their escape from Vesuvius in great detail and with vigorous arm movements.

Mordecai and Rectina, both in dark blue, sat next to each other. They were discussing useful ointments for baby skin irritation.

Nubia sat straight in her prettiest yellow silk tunic. She was demonstrating some fingering on her cherrywood flute to Aristo.

On Jonathan's left sat Flavia. She was wearing her best pale-blue tunic and Nubia had arranged her hair. A strand had already escaped and Flavia kept brushing it out of her eyes as she told Felix about how she and Sisyphus had discovered the tunnels in the Golden House.

"Jonathan," purred a voice in his ear. "Is it true you saved the Emperor from an assassin?"

He turned to look at Pulchra and smiled.

"We all had a part in it."

"Will you tell me about it?" She was wearing a pink silk tunic and pink ribbons were braided into her yellow hair. She smelled of lemon blossom.

"Some day," said Jonathan. "Not yet. But I would like to play you a song I wrote."

"You've learned to play!" Pulchra opened her blue eyes in delight and clapped her hands.

"Let's say I'm learning." Jonathan smiled as he reached behind his cushion and lifted up his bass lyre.

"A Syrian barbiton!" Felix sat up with interest and Jonathan remembered he was a keen musician. "Where did you get it?"

"My uncle bought it in Rome, and he gave it to me," said Jonathan. "He taught me how to play, but so far I can only play one song. Would you like to hear it?"

"Yes!" everyone cried.

Jonathan settled the instrument and gripped the smooth bulb of the sound box between his bare feet. Already it felt right, as if it were part of him.

"I wrote this song myself," he said, looking around at them. "I call it 'Penelope's Loom.'"

Jonathan closed his eyes and found his heartbeat. Then he speeded it up and began to play.

FINIS

ARISTO'S SCROLL

alabastron (al - uh - **bas** - tron)
a small ceramic perfume jar, designed to look as if it is made of alabaster

amphitheater (**am** - fee - theater)
an oval-shaped stadium for watching gladiator shows, beast fights, and mock sea-battles; the Colosseum in Rome is the most famous one

amphora (am - **for** - uh)
large clay storage jar for holding wine, oil, or grain

Aramaic (air - uh - **may** - ik)
closely related to Hebrew, it was the main language of first-century Jews

atrium (**eh** - tree - um)
the reception room in larger Roman homes, often with sky light and pool

ballista (buh - **list** - uh)
a type of Roman catapult used for hurling stones and other missiles

barbiton (**bar** - bi - ton)
a kind of Greek bass lyre, but there is no evidence for a "Syrian barbiton"

basilica (buh - **sill** - i - kuh)
Roman building in the forum which housed law courts, offices, and cells

Berenice (bare - uh - **neece**)
a beautiful Jewish queen, from the family of Herod, aged about fifty when this story takes place

Britannicus (Bri - **tan** - ick - uss)
son and heir of the Emperor Claudius, he was poisoned by Nero

cicada (sick - **ah** - duh)
an insect like a grasshopper that chirrs during the day

Circus Maximus (**sir** - kuss **max** - i - muss)
long racetrack in the center of Rome, near the Palatine Hill

Corinth (**kor** - inth)
Greek port town with a large Jewish population

cryptoporticus (krip - toe - **por** - tick - uss)
means "secret corridor" in Greek, usually a long inner corridor

Cyclops (**sigh** - klops)
a mythical monster with a single eye in the center of his forehead

denarii (den - **are** - ee)
more than one denarius, a silver coin. A denarius equals four sestercii.

Domitian (duh - **mish** - an)
the Emperor Titus's younger brother, twenty-nine when this story takes place

ecce! (**ek** - kay)
Latin word meaning "behold!" or "look!"

Feast of Trumpets
the Jewish New Year (Rosh Hashannah), so called because the shofar is blown

forum (**for** - um)
ancient marketplace and civic center in Roman towns

Fortuna (for - **tew** - nuh)
the goddess of good luck and success

freedwoman (**freed** - woman)

a female slave who has been granted freedom

fullers

ancient laundry and clothmakers; they used human urine to bleach wool

Hebrew (**hee** - brew)

holy language of the Old Testament, spoken by (religious) Jews in the first century

Herculaneum (herk - you - **lane** - ee - um)

the "town of Hercules" at the foot of Vesuvius; it was buried by mud in the eruption of A.D. 79 and has now been partly excavated

Ides (eyedz)

the thirteenth day of most months in the Roman calendar (including September); in March, July, October and May the Ides occur on the fifteenth day of the month.

insula (**in** - syu - luh)

a city block; literally, an island

Jewish calendar

the Jewish calendar is a lunar one, based on the cycles of the moon, unlike the Roman calendar (and our modern one) based on cycles of the sun. Jewish months always begin on the day of the new moon. The fourteenth therefore always occurs on the full moon. Also, the new day starts in the evening.

Josephus (jo - **see** - fuss)

Jewish commander who surrendered to Vespasian, became Titus's freedman, and wrote *The Jewish War*, an account of the Jewish revolt, in seven volumes.

Judaea (jew - **dee** - uh)

ancient province of the Roman Empire; modern Israel

Juno (**jew** - no)

queen of the Roman gods and wife of the god Jupiter

Kalends

the Kalends mark the first day of the month in the Roman calendar

kohl (kole)
dark powder used to darken eyelids or outline eyes

Ludi Romani (**loo** - dee ro - **mah** - nee)
two-week Roman festival held in September and celebrated with chariot races

Messiah (mess - **eye** - uh)
the Hebrew word for Christ; both words mean "anointed" or "chosen" one

Neapolis (nee - **ap** - o - liss)
a large city in the south of Italy near Vesuvius; modern Naples

Nero (**near** - oh)
wicked Emperor; built the Golden House after the great fire of Rome in A.D. 64

Odysseus (uh - **diss** - yooss)
Greek hero who fought against Troy; his journey home took twenty years

Odyssey (**odd** - iss - ee)
Homer's Greek epic poem about the adventures of Odysseus on his way home

Oppian Hill (**opp** - ee - an)
part of the Esquiline Hill in Rome and site of Nero's Golden House

Ostia (**oss** - tee - uh)
the port of ancient Rome and hometown of Flavia Gemina

Palatine (**pal** - uh - tine)
one of the seven hills of Rome; the greenest and most pleasant; the site of successive imperial palaces (the word "palace" comes from "Palatine")

papyrus (puh - **pie** - russ)
the cheapest writing material, made of Egyptian reeds

Pausilypon (pow - **sill** - ip - on)
modern Posillipo, a coastal town near Naples

Pella (**pell** - uh)
an ancient city near the Jordan River where the Jewish believers in Jesus (the first Christians) sought refuge during the Jewish Wars

Penelope (pen - **ell** - uh - pee)
faithful wife of Odysseus, who waited twenty years for him to return from Troy

pergola (**purr** - go - luh)
an arbor or walkway made of plants trained to grow over a trellis

peristyle (**perry** - style)
a columned walkway around an inner garden or courtyard

Pliny (**plin** - ee) (the Elder)
famous Roman author; died in the eruption of Vesuvius

Pollux
one of the famous twins of Greek mythology

Polyphemus (polly - **fee** - muss)
the Cyclops whom Odysseus blinded in order to escape being devoured

Pompeii (pom - **pay**)
a prosperous coastal town buried by the eruption of Vesuvius in A.D. 79

psaltery (**salt** - ree)
a kind of Jewish lyre or harp

Puteoli (poo - tee - **oh** - lee)
modern Pozzuoli, ancient Rome's great commercial port on the Bay of Naples

Sabbath (**sab** - uth)
the Jewish day of rest, counted from Friday evening to Saturday evening

sardonyx (sar - don - iks)

semiprecious stone; usually orange or brown, sometimes streaked with white

scroll (skrole)
: a papyrus or parchment "book," unrolled from side to side as it was read.

sestercii (sess - **tur** - see)
: more than one sestercius, a brass coin. Four sestercii equal a denarius.

Sextus Propertius (**sex** - tuss pro - **purr** - shuss)
: an elegant Roman poet who was a contemporary of Virgil and Ovid

shalom (shah-**lome**)
: the Hebrew word for "peace"; can also mean "hello" or "good-bye"

shofar (**show** - far)
: a special trumpet made from a ram's horn, used to announce Jewish holy days

sica (**seek** - uh)
: sickle-shaped dagger used by Jewish assassins (sicarii) in the first century A.D.

signet ring (**sig** - net ring)
: ring with an image carved in it to be pressed into wax and used as a personal seal

Stabia (sta -**bee** - uh)
: modern Castellamare di Stabia, a town south of Pompeii

stylus (**stile** - us)
: a metal, wood, or ivory tool for writing on wax tablets

sukkah (**sook**-uh)
: a shelter woven of branches for the Feast of Tabernacles

Sukkoth (sook - **ot**)
: another name for the Feast of Tabernacles, one of the great festivals of the Jewish year; for eight days Jews eat and sleep in shelters ("sukkoth")

Surrentum (sir - **wren** - tum)

modern Sorrento, a pretty harbor town south of Vesuvius

Titus (**tie** - tuss)

new Emperor of Rome and son of Vespasian, aged thirty-nine when this story takes place (full name: Titus Flavius Vespasianus)

toga (**toe** - ga)

a blanketlike outer garment, worn by freeborn men and boys

Torah (**tor**-uh)

Hebrew word meaning "law" or "instruction." It can refer to the first five Books of the Bible or to the entire Old Testament.

triclinium (trick - **lin** - ee - um)

ancient Roman dining room, usually with three couches to recline on

trigon (**try** - gon)

ball game in which three players stand at different points of an imaginary triangle and throw a ball to each other as fast and hard as they can; you lose if you drop it

tunic (**tew** - nic)

a piece of clothing like a big T-shirt; children often wore a long-sleeved one

Vespasian (vess - **pay** - zhun)

Roman Emperor who died three months before this story begins; Titus's father

Vesuvius (vuh - **soo** - vee - yus)

the volcano near Naples which erupted on August 24 A.D. 79

wax tablet

a wax-covered rectangle of wood used for making notes

Yom Kippur (yom ki-poor)

the Day of Atonement, holiest and most solemn day in the Jewish calendar, when Jews fast for twenty-four hours to ask God's forgiveness for the sins of the past year. It ends the ten Days of Awe, which begin on the Jewish new year.

THE LAST SCROLL

In the spring of A.D. 70, nine and a half years before this story takes place, four Roman legions surrounded the rebellious city of Jerusalem. The commander was Titus, son of Rome's new Emperor, Vespasian. Jerusalem should have withstood the siege for years, but weakened by the fighting of those inside, it fell in months. Those few months were among the most terrible in the history of the Jewish people. Thousands were crucified as they tried to escape. Those who remained in the city suffered terrible famine. Finally, the Temple of God was destroyed, Jerusalem razed to the ground, and the survivors killed or enslaved.

Titus returned to Rome in triumph with thousands of Jewish slaves. It is probable that many of them were put to work building Vespasian's new amphitheater. This monument came to be known as the Colosseum, after the colossal statue of Nero that stood nearby.

Nero had died a year before the fall of Jerusalem. His opulent Golden House only survived another thirty-five years before it became the site of Trajan's baths. Nobody knows exactly what it was used for during those years. Today, if you visit Rome, you can still visit part of the Golden House. There you will see painted rooms, a long cryptoporticus, an octagonal pavilion, and a "cave of the Cyclops."

Simeon, Susannah, and Rizpah were not real people. Titus, Domitian, Josephus, and Berenice were. You can read more about them in history books.

Book I:
THE THIEVES OF OSTIA

The year is A.D. 79. The place is Ostia, the port of Rome. Flavia Gemina, a Roman sea captain's daughter, is about to embark on a thrilling adventure.

The theft of her father's signet ring leads her to three extraordinary people—Jonathan the Jewish boy next door, Nubia the African slave girl, and Lupus, the mute beggar boy—who become her friends. Their investigations take them to the harbor, the forum, and the tombs of the dead, as they try to discover who is killing the dogs of Ostia, and why.

Book II:
THE SECRETS OF VESUVIUS

Flavia, Jonathan, Nubia, and Lupus sail to the Bay of Naples to spend the rest of their summer with Flavia's uncle, who lives near Pompeii. They are soon absorbed in trying to solve a riddle that may lead them to a great treasure.

Meanwhile, tremors shake the ground, animals behave strangely, and people dream of impending doom. One of the worst natural disasters of all time is about to happen—the eruption of Mount Vesuvius. The four friends are in terrible danger!

Book III:
THE PIRATES OF POMPEII

It's late August A.D. 79. The Roman world is reeling from the eruption of Mount Vesuvius. Volcanic ash covers the land, sunsets are blood-red, and the sea gives up corpses of the dead.

At a makeshift camp south of Stabia, hundreds of refugees from the city of Vesuvius try to come to terms with the disaster. When children begin to go missing from the camp, Flavia Gemina and her friends Jonathan, Nubia, and Lupus investigate a powerful and charismatic man known as the Patron.

The Pirates of Pompeii leads the four friends on a dangerous mission where they encounter pirates, slave-dealers, and death.